The .... -

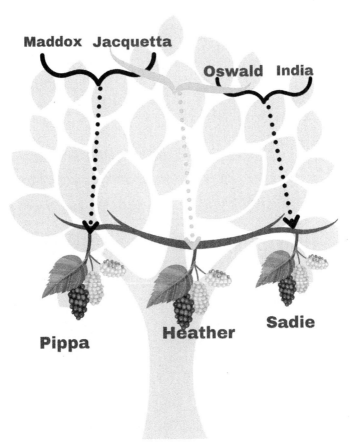

My Half-Sister's Half-Sister
Samantha Henthorn

©Samantha Henthorn 2021
All rights reserved.

This book is dedicated to my sister-in-law, Kerry Marshall

Here we go round the mulberry bush,
The mulberry bush,
The mulberry bush.
Here we go round the mulberry bush
on a cold and frosty morning.

Unknown female inmate, HMP Wakefield
(19th century)

Before

My feet feel sort of cold, and the hall smells like washing powder and old oranges. Mummy queues up at the bottle tombola, and that's when I look down.

No... no... please... Why didn't Mummy tell me? I've come out to the school fair wearing my bedroom slippers. I try and put one foot on top of the other but that only draws attention. Stop it. I look across the room, and I notice that girl from swimming. Why does this kind of thing always happen to me?

I hate swim class... wet hair on a cold day and my see-through costume. I hate it, can't do it, and the swim teacher is grumpy and tells us off. She reckons that we should know how to swim at our age; *it's ridiculous.* I swallowed chlorine from up my nose when my head went under. I tried to stretch my arms and legs out, but the pool was just wet air. I grabbed the side and tried to walk along with the movement of the water. It's like I'm there now; I just can't do it.

This girl never seems bothered that she can't swim. I think she is a year older than me and from a different school. Different, except we all get banded together. The different ones, the ones who can't swim.

She's chewing bubble gum (banned at our house, definitely banned during swim class), and I wish Mummy had one of her long skirts on to hide my feet.

'Jacqui!' the girl's mum puts a cigarette out in her hand.

'India,' Mummy says. She does not look pleased; she has the same look on her face when I ask to use the bathroom at the shops.

'Our two are at the same swim class, then?' India wears an eye patch on her left eye, and the girl pops her bubble gum bubble in my face (at least she hasn't noticed my feet).

The smell in the school hall changes and all the parents try not to notice. I've smelt this smell before, sort of like flowers and being naughty at the same time... It stinks, but it's nice too. It belongs to a man with red-rimmed eyes and nearly a beard. 'How's Heather?' the smell says. Mummy bristles her shoulders. Heather is my big sister, and she's late coming home from university. The girl chews her gum.

'I believe you can't swim either,' the girl's mum says to me. I open my mouth to say something, but I get a tickle in my throat.

'I think we both know they won't drown,' Mummy does a laugh that isn't a laugh because what she said was not a joke. Then we walk away, which is terrible because Mummy has given up her place in the queue. I had my eye on a bottle of Ribena (banned at our house), and Mummy had her eye on a bottle of brandy. At least I got away without anyone noticing what I'm wearing on my feet.

The girl looks straight at me and pops another bubble right in my face. 'Nice slippers,' she says.

Chapter One

'Epiphany! Epiphany!'

It is funny how memories pop into your head from years ago, like a flashback that you're trying to forget. I often wish I could turn my brain off just to get some peace.

I should try harder to wake up and avoid being half asleep because that's when these thoughts usually intrude.

'Epiphany! Epiphany!' Mummy shouts from downstairs. I hear her key turn halfway, and she's muttering to herself, inviting all kinds to unlock the door to my flat.

'Epiphany, what's wrong with your front door?' Mummy shouts.

Yes. Epiphany is my name – Pippa for short, strictly Pippa for short. I don't mind Pip but definitely not Epiphany. When Mummy was pregnant with my older sister, she intended to name her Hazel. Right up to the last minute, Hazel. Then a midwife told her that Hazel is a witch's name, and this put her off. So, Mummy chose the name Heather. It suits her because my sister's eyes shine hazel when she's excited.

Some years later, Mummy was pregnant again

(by a different man) and had an epiphany. Literally, she had an Epiphany. I hate my name. It isn't a name; it's a noun, and I never use it. Always, I introduce myself as Pippa; always Pippa (like Heather's Pippa doll). My boyfriend doesn't even know what my full name is. I'm frumpy, fair, nearly forty, and I live in the upstairs quarters of a pub that remains closed after the lockdown ended.

I often wonder when I'm going to have an epiphany.

'I need you to drive me to the vet's, Epiphany. It's Patrice. She's not eating again.'

Mummy has managed to enter my flat. I don't know why she can't drive herself or wait for Heather; it's not like she has to work. One year, Heather was late returning home from university at Christmas. We were worried sick, I remember because I was about eleven at the time, or ten, maybe. When Heather finally arrived home, she announced that her studies had ended. She now knew all she needed to know because she had met her husband. Heather introduced us to Rhys; they had both decided what they wanted from life (each other). Four children later (all soothed by a bra-less Heather jogging prams around a large garden), Heather and Rhys are still happy together. I've no idea what they do for a living, but they are loaded.

'Mummy, I'm working at the office today. You know I don't like to be late.' It was as though I hadn't spoken.

'Your front door is sticking again. Come on, get dressed. You have plenty of time to run Patrice to the vet.'

It's not really my front door. It's an interior door inside my mother's pub, The Peacock. I have lived in the flat upstairs since I left home. I didn't go far; Mummy lives across the road with her husband.

'Why don't you drive Patrice to the vet? Hang on; you are coming, aren't you?' I spoke as I zipped my skirt.

'I've got to stay and supervise the workmen,' Mummy's eyes widened. Need she say more? Workmen are always doing something to her house. Always.

'Can't John do it?' I try not to roll my eyes, but it's no good.

'No, he's still asleep,' Mummy is halfway out of the door, minus Patrice's kitty carrier.

'Mummy! I don't know what to say to the vet. Patrice is your cat, and I don't know what tests she had done last time she was there.'

'Fine,' Mummy grabs Patrice. 'I was going to ask one of the builders to pop over and have a look at the snag in your lock. But, if you're going to be selfish, Epiphany, I shall escort you to the vet's.' We leave without a snag and without saying goodbye to Ben.

I've never had the same luck as Heather with men; they never seem to look at me and realise they have found what they want in life. Except when I met Ben, I proved the rule wrong that a man won't be serious about you if you sleep with them on the first night. This year, on Valentine's Day, he got me a card. Men only buy cards for women they are serious about (even though this one included a lockdown joke; *'Can't wait to see less of you!'*).

Patrice does seem to frequent the vet's regularly these days. I wonder how old she is. Mind you, when I was a child, my year of birth was up for debate. Mummy has a legendary fondness for spirits, and one year rolled into another for her. Heather saved me because she remembered watching (and relating to) *The Growing Pains of Adrian Mole* when I was a baby. We had to wait until Google allowed us to confirm the year – up until then, I had been pegged as a year younger than I am.

And if that isn't enough, I don't know how old Mummy is; no one does. Her age jumps around like hailstones on a patio. I do not know anyone else with such a secretive mother. Apart from Heather, she doesn't know Mummy's age either and no amount of remembering televised comedy dramas can help us.

Mummy pokes her fingers through the gate of the kitty carrier. 'It's alright, Patrice. The vet will probably just tell me off for not giving you enough variety in your diet.'

My mother, Jacquetta (always Jacquetta, NEVER Jacqui), has rarely been without a cat. Or 'sans feline,' as she puts it; I think she knows time is running out for Patrice. And I think I have just found out why Mummy can't drive this morning. When I fastened my seatbelt, I smelt the distinctive smell of arabica, bananas and burning wood. Or Irish coffee, American style (as I put it).

After receiving unsolicited advice from one of Mummy's builders about how to reverse my car out of The Peacock's driveway, we set off for the vet's. Unfortunately, we still have to queue outside because of the restrictions. And soon, on this cold and frosty morning, Mummy is openly crying on Manchester Road.

Chapter Two

They were tears of joy, relief, and release (but mostly tears of performance). With all those pet owners and cars zooming past (relishing in the buzz of rush hour), Mummy could not resist bringing the drama. After a diagnosis of acute rhinitis, Patrice was treated with antibiotics and kept in overnight for intravenous fluids.

Mummy would not be reassured unless she was paying for every scrap of advice the vet could offer.

'My poor little fur baby, no wonder she wasn't eating. She couldn't smell her food,' Mummy looked at me. She's about to say something else. I really should be driving to work. I'm already late. 'Cats smell their food to check that it's safe. Very clever, aren't you, Patrice... oh! I forgot, she isn't here, hmmm no one to keep me company all night.' Mummy pulls her hand back from the place she thought she was stroking her cat. She looks very distressed. She isn't, though. I can tell.

'Wake John up, Mummy,' I remind my mother she has a husband. Then, despite being sans feline, I leave her at the side of the road and turn my car around.

Every morning, I pass the library. When I was

a child (during the no age years), I quite fancied being a librarian. All the books... Today, it's a good job that I work in an office. No readers need their books stamped... I have no customers or prior shift workers anxious to leave and get to their beds, so it shouldn't matter what time I arrive at work. If lockdown taught us anything, a flexible approach is essential. I just hope my boss (and Karen, the receptionist) agree.

The... establishment underneath my office is a tattoo parlour. For the past few weeks (probably to boost customer interest after lockdown), they have an advertisement in the window 'TAROT CARD READINGS EVERY THURSDAY AFTERNOON'. I must book in.

No one comments regarding my tardiness until Karen's face approaches my desk later in the afternoon. 'A call came through for you on the reception line,' her face mask gives her no cover. 'I took a message because you can't handle my mouthpiece, as you know.'

'What is it then?' I had to ask because Karen looks like she has a point to make.

'And I can't put calls through to you anymore. Your line is bust,' Karen's face says, *and you were late this morning*. 'It was your boyfriend. He said to tell you that your sister is at your flat.'

That was weird. Why is Heather at my house? Ben doesn't need to phone me at work to tell me my sister is visiting; she's always at Mummy's over the road. Always. And why can I smell Karen's bad breath even though she's wearing a face mask? Weird.

After a long day (I made the hour up), it is time to go home and see Heather. Although I could really do without this tonight, I haven't managed to message Mummy to ask how Patrice is. Karen's eyes were on me for the rest of the day. I wouldn't mind, but she sits with her back to me on the other side of the partition. I've got a feeling the cat will be fine at the vet's; she still has most of her nine lives.

As I pull into The Peacock's driveway, Ben appears to be on his way out. 'Your sister called round,' he tells me what I already know.

'No hello?' we closed-mouth kiss on the lips.

'I've got to dash, sorry. Cass has a problem with her washing machine,' Ben says. I've never seen him move so fast when Cassandra needs a favour.

'Again?' I try for breezy, but I know my face is bitchy.

'Yes, you *know* her husband is working away.'

'And she's got you wrapped around her little finger,' (I whispered that to myself). 'I know, I meant, poor thing. I hope you can fix it.' Our faces are lit only by the car park lanterns positioned at the root of old oak trees.

'Right, see you later,' Ben says.

I sigh as I climb the stairs to my flat. I wonder what Heather wants.

My big chair faces my big back window, where a woman sits with her back to me. Her long, slender legs (covered in shiny black leggings – the kind I cannot wear without ripping a hole in my pride) dangle over the side of the opposite chair arm. My eyes follow her legs all the way up to her coat. It is exactly like the grey fox fur blouson that Freddie Mercury wore in the *Killer Queen* video. It is exactly like the (faux) fox fur blouson I donated to charity six months ago. Not because I didn't like it, I just couldn't get it to suit me. She hasn't taken the coat off. Either Ben didn't make her feel welcome, or she isn't staying. Also, this woman is not my sister.

She must have sensed my presence (probably because I gasped) and swung her long legs and her heeled biker boots round to face me.

'Epiphany!' she threw her arms out wide to hug me and popped a bubble gum bubble.

'Sadie,' I returned her greeting with my typical hesitancy.

Chapter Three

'It's Pippa, strictly Pippa.' It's all about boundaries when you're telling someone your name. 'No one ever calls me Epiphany... sorry.'

'Okay, sister,' a smile spreads across Sadie's full lips. She's not my sister, though; she's my half-sister's half-sister.

'This is a surprise... a nice surprise.' I did not know what to say. After work, especially if Ben leaves me, and especially during an exceptionally frosty winter, I like to go to bed not long after arriving home. But now, there is a glamorously beautiful person chewing gum in my living room – and she thinks she's related to me.

'Were you expecting the Pocahontas of Pendle?' Sadie grins.

'What! You can't say that!' she meant Heather, who lives in Pendle and does look a bit like she's descended from America's past.

'Why not? Look.' Sadie performs a centre parting in her lengthy black hair and two plaits appear (in record time). 'Heather and I have our dad's genes. You know as well as I do that Oswald's great-great, however-many-grandads was one of the Salford Sioux, so if *I* was teased at school about it, then it's fine for me to say it about Heather.'

Teased? Is she joking? This woman is the living embodiment of all things beautiful. I challenge any female to see what I'm looking at now and not covet at least one part of her. And Heather (from the same gene pool) is *not bad* either, whereas I'm stuck with industry bred Lancastrian thunder thighs, watery blue eyes, and premature jowls. I'd better say something and stop looking at her. Yes, stop staring, Epiphany.

'I like your coat. And your leggings, I like your boots too.'

Sadie stops twirling her plaits to admire her own feet.

'I had a blouson just like that,' I said.

'A blouson?' Sadie's mouth turned up at the corners, and when she said 'blouson', she put on a voice.

'You know. A jacket that looks like a blouse. I couldn't get mine to suit me... like you can, I suppose.'

'It's just the way I put on our clothes,' said Sadie.

'Pardon?'

'I mean my clothes,' Sadie hugs the faux fox fur around herself. 'Let's have a drink, Pippa.'

It was as though I had not breathed out for a while. Sadie followed me into the kitchen, and I ran the tap for the kettle. 'I haven't seen you since...'

'Swim class?' Sadie made speech marks and

rolled her eyes. She laughed at the same time as she spoke, and it sounded as good as the first glug of wine falling into the glass. 'What are you doing with the kettle, Pippa?'

'Making us a drink, do you want tea or coffee?' I pulled two mugs down from the cupboard; we *will* have something wet, warm, and non-alcoholic.

'Neither! I want vodka. Vodka and diet coke... it's all I drink. Besides, I heard...' Sadie's voice trailed off and my shoulders flinched.

'You only drink vodka and diet coke... ever? That's all you *ever* drink?' I know what Sadie 'heard', and I'm not going there.

'When I'm in a pub, I mean like we are now, Pippa. Anyway, we need a drink,' Sadie gave me a conspiratorial look behind her long black eyelashes.

'Do we?' I anxiously twirled dry blond frizz around my finger.

'Yes, you've had a hard day at work, doing sums, haven't you?'

How does Sadie know what I do?

'Fine,' Sadie raised her hands in surrender. 'Coffee for me, please.'

'How do you take it?'

'Hot, like me. And as black as my soul,' Sadie laughed a *joking-not-joking* laugh and linked my arm with hers. I can tell exactly what she's thinking.

I am at a loss as to why Sadie is here. She has taken her coat off now but still has the gum in her mouth. We are talking like long, lost friends. Despite Sadie's loyalty to vodka, the coffee has been replaced by a bottle of wine. Weirdly, this had already chilled in the fridge.

I don't drink... anymore. I found out a while ago – during a particularly thirsty summer that I'm allergic to alcohol. Spirits, wine, beer, cider, they all have a funny effect on me. Do not try and tempt me with liqueur chocolate at Christmas, and do not dare come anywhere near me with that popular fizzy poison. It's not like a bee sting or a nut allergy. My face and extremities do not swell up until I suffer respiratory arrest. It's worse, but it's not as bad...

All I know is that Mummy gets to have a restorative nip whenever she likes. Why can't I be a closet habitual drinker? Like Sadie's glamour, it is all or nothing with me. Call off the emergency services; a bottle of wine has been opened, but I can't be persuaded that easily.

'None for me actually,' I put my hand over one of the wine glasses that Sadie has adopted for us.

'Aww,' Sadie pouts.

'I've got work in the morning. I could drink tonic, though, tonic and ice in a wine glass.' Ever the people pleaser, I don't want Sadie to feel unwelcome at this party (or whatever this is). 'I just need to nip downstairs to borrow some of those fancy tonics from the bar.'

Chapter Four

I admit I have been 'borrowing' from the pub more frequently during the last year. I presume that sundries such as tonic, diet coke, and crisps have a shelf life. I have conned myself into believing that my acts of petty theft are really an act of kindness. When the pub reopens, no punter shall fall foul of a flat mixer or a stale crisp.

'Here we are... oh, I see you've already started,' I was a bit out of breath when I reached the top of the stairs.

'Pippa, I'm dying to know...What on *earth* you are doing with that loser.' Sadie has made herself at home. Her boots are off, her feet are on the table, and she's insulting my boyfriend.

'Ben?' I say, feigning injury.

'It's just... I was surprised to see that someone *like you* would be dating... someone like *that*,' Sadie's fancy manicured hand is on my forearm. We both sip our drinks, her hair is glorious, and her face is alive. 'It's none of my business, but does he have a massive willy?'

We both explode laughing, and the liquid goes up our noses.

'Can I tell you something?' What am I doing? Loose lips sink ships, as Mummy always said. I see a flicker of hazel in Sadie's eyes, just like my sister.

'You can tell me anything. What's yours is mine,' Sadie drains her glass. Seemingly, she's as much of a lightweight as I was.

'Did Ben seem in a rush to go out before?' I ask.

'Yes, yes he did!' Sadie's eyes were as wide as the glass she just filled.

'There's this woman. Actually, she used to be a friend of mine until... she unfriended me. Now, she's latched on to Ben, and she's always asking him for things. Even during the lockdown, he was round at her house loads.'

'What? How did you know he was at her house? Did you follow him... like you did that time?'

'He told me.' I cut Sadie off mid-sentence. I like that she's an eager audience, but how does she know about all my indiscretions? I have heard nothing from Sadie since swim class.

'He TOLD you? What the hell!' Sadie is affronted.

'Yes, he would say *Cass has a problem with her washing machine. Cass's car has broken down; she needs a lift to the shops. You know her husband is working away*.' I don't know why, but I put a funny voice on, mimicking my prodigal boyfriend.

Sadie almost spat her wine out. 'Wait, wait, what? He was going round there to play house? I thought you meant he told you when he was *cheating* on you!' Sadie smiled but shook her head and hair from side to side.

'No, just doing her favours. All the time,

though. But it was lockdown; her germs became my germs because Ben was bringing them home.'

'The dirty bastard!' Sadie adjusts her shoulders to fighting talk.

'I think he's having an emotional affair with her.'

'I think he's having an *affair* with her,' Sadie sympathises. 'Wait, do you mean *Cassandra*?'

'Yes.' Does Sadie know everyone?

'Oh my God, Epiphany! What are you worried about that fucking five-head for? Unless Ben has a thing for skinny women with massive foreheads and no personality, you have nothing to worry about.'

I feel better already.

'The thing is, I don't think he's sleeping with her. It's just that he puts her first. When I look around this flat, there are loads of little DIY jobs that I've asked him to do, and he hasn't because he's been too busy doing things for Cassandra.'

'Jobs?' Sadie said.

'Yes, the other day I took the shower caddy off to clean it, and the whole thing fell down.'

'So?'

'I'd asked him to fix it for me, and he didn't do a proper job.'

'That's marriage for you,' Sadie throws one of her plaits over her shoulder.

'We're not married.' I'm pretty sure I won't be getting married ever; I've been a bridesmaid twice for Mummy and once for Heather already.

'No, but you're acting like you are married. Do your own DIY jobs, Pippa, don't be like Cassandra, falling apart because her husband isn't there,' Sadie has moved on to pep-talk. 'So, do you think... is Ben sleeping with Cassandra? Or is Ben making you think he is so that you will change your behaviour? OR worse, is *Cassandra* seeking revenge for 'unfriending' her, or whatever it was?' Sadie is so insightful about the dynamics of twisted monogamy.

'*She* unfriended me,' I sigh and wonder how Sadie knows Cassandra– everyone knows about her husband working away, it seems.

'Why did she fall out with you?' Sadie sounds curious.

'It's a long story...' I want to tell her that I couldn't understand why Cassandra had cut me off (I'm adorable). But I need to be careful here; I don't want to bore Sadie and scare her away.

'I've got all night,' Sadie picks up the wine bottle. The *almost finished* status dangles like a price tag.

'I've got more wine... downstairs.'

'Hold those little tonic bottles this time,' Sadie shouts down to me as I rob the pub.

As I select another bottle of wine (better make it non-sparkling this time), I think about explaining my contretemps with Cassandra. The thing is, what happened will make me sound like I'm paranoid. She was a bully at school and an emotional vampire afterwards. Everything was on Cassandra's terms, I had to bend over backwards to appease her, yet she would make excuse after excuse to turn down my invitations. First, she would lie about one of her children being ill (people should never lie about their children). Then, she would say that she had no funds (yet I would see her going out to an expensive place with her other friends on the same night).

After *it* happened... she went after Ben. He is an easy target – a sucker for a damsel in distress. Except Cassandra is no persecuted maiden, she's a femme fatale, and Ben is vulnerable to her manipulations.

I catch a glimpse of myself in the backsplash mirror. Why can't I be Bathsheba Everdene? Instead, I am Tess Durbeyfield; I'd better make it concise when I go back upstairs.

'Have you got any food? I'm starving.' Sadie has loosened her hair from its heritage knots and sits cross-legged in front of the fireplace.

'Of course,' I slide over an under-counter box of posh crisps.

'Fabulous,' Sadie rips open the bag like a professional snack server. 'So, start from the beginning. First of all, how did you know she'd fallen out with you?'

'I told you, Cassandra unfriended *me*,' none of this is my fault... I've got to make that clear.

'Yes, you said, but how exactly.'

'On Facebook...'

'What! Wait, Facebook wasn't a thing until *after* we left school. Especially in your case, being a year younger.'

'This was recent,' I blush. I desperately want to correct Sadie about my age, but it's more important to convey my wounds without making myself look at fault.

'Did you ask her why?'

'I didn't want to... at first.'

'So, how did Ben start following Cassandra's breadcrumbs?'

'She got rid of me but kept Ben as a friend. Then she started being his *best* friend on social media, you know the type, always commenting on everything he posted.'

'Did he show you?'

'No! I was looking at Ben's profile.'

Sadie runs her finger around the rim of her glass.

'In the end, I confronted Cassandra by pretending to be Ben on Facebook. And do you know what she said?' I can feel my wine allergy flaring up just by being in proximity with a bottle of the stuff. Cassandra has turned me into a boring person who makes everyone feel uncomfortable by asking rhetorical questions. Yet, Sadie appears to be listening. 'She said it was my fault, that it was my entire fault. But that wasn't fair. She was the one who cut me off, not the other way round.'

'Shh,' Sadie says. I don't know why my head is

on her lap. 'You know... if you did cut her off, it's only because she handed you the scissors... Cassandra's a real bitch,' Sadie smirks in opposition.

'The only time she's spoken to me since was when she told me she could take Ben off me.' I've got to get my point across. I'm not paranoid.

'Take him off you? Is Ben a possession? ... Do you know what I think?' Sadie rests her chin on her fist.

'What?' I need to know.

'She's playing Ben, and Ben's playing you. Cassandra obviously feels threatened by you, so she makes out that she could take your man.'

I catch a glimpse of my own reflection in the big back window. I'm not buying Sadie's spin.

'Are you feeling trapped?' Sadie stretches her arms over her head.

'You said trapped.' Is she reading *my* mind now?

'You are, you're trapped in this house that used to be a pub, you've been incarcerated for an entire year because of the restrictions, and those two have done a bad thing – she has used him to screw you.' I hear Sadie's meaning the third time, and her arms widen. 'I need to know the whole story. How did you meet Ben?'

This is awesome; the gratitude I feel right now is immense. Finally, after all this time, someone is listening to me. 'We met because he was working here, in the pub.'

Sadie raised an eyebrow.

'Yes, he was one of the bar staff. I presume he will be when the pub reopens.' I wonder if Sadie has noticed that The Peacock is the only pub within a fifty-mile radius that remains closed. That's a lot of pubs with one less competitor.

'Don't tell me, Ben gradually moved in? Pippa! This gets better and better. It's a good job I turned up when I did...' Sadie is as engrossed in my pity party as she is in her glass of wine. I need to get the focus off Ben and back to Cassandra. I feel stupid for letting Ben slide into my life. He's a lot younger than me, and really, we have nothing in common. It was one night, one night when Ben asked me where my husband was. I told him I was single, he said he didn't believe me. That was all it took. I know that I was probably a convenience to him. And yes, I have worried that if the pub doesn't start trading soon, he will move on to another job and another woman.

'I did find a love letter that Cassandra sent to Ben.' I offer up the evidence to support my claim.

'This isn't a love letter!' Sadie flips the envelope over. There is nothing inside, but it is how the envelope is written.

DEAR ᗡEN, DO NOT OPEN THIS UNTIL YOUR BIRTHDAY, LOVE *C XX*

'Do you see?' I am convinced.

'It's just an envelope from his birthday card.' Sadie sounds sober again, and I sound like the unhinged one.

'No, but she's made the 'B' of Ben into a heart, plus she's signed her name with her initial... Who does that?'

'Maybe she thinks she's the only 'C' in the world. What did Ben say about it?' Sadie flips the envelope right across the coffee table.

'Oh, oh, Ben had plenty to say,' I take another swig of my neat tonic water. 'He said the card was from me; that I signed it but forgot to finish making the 'C' into an 'E'. Ben's playing mind games. He doesn't even know my name is Epiphany. He thinks I'm called Pippa, just Pippa.' My posture is triumphant, but I sound nuts.

'We should keep this,' Sadie retrieves the envelope and folds it into her handbag as though we are in cahoots together.

'Thank you,' I love this sister; we are simpatico.

Chapter Five

The last thing I remember about yesterday evening was Sadie telling me that I look tired. Retelling the whole Ben and Cassandra story sounded flimsy, I know, and it drained me. I was tired, I suppose, and I'm still half asleep now.

After all these years, Sadie is still chewing gum, but the rest of her is a raven-haired phoenix. Sadie is Mary Lennox's missing key, and she replaced Ben last night sleeping next to me with sisterly comfort. And where I can *never* smell perfume on myself, Sadie's bouquet fills my senses with cloves, mint, and apple.

I am too hot and too cold. I turn over, and I am alone. Where did Sadie go? Olfactory hallucinations are rarer than visual ones, apparently... I remember now; Ben sent me a text late last night with some excuse or other about staying over at Cassandra's.

Shit! I've got to get up; I promised to drive Mummy back to the vet's to collect Patrice on my way to work. I'm many things, but I'm not unreliable. I can't let Mummy down.

Like in the good old days, I'm dressed in yesterday's clothes. There is nothing like waking up in your makeup to save time. But I won't risk protecting others from my death breath with a face mask, so I reach for the mouthwash. This is the way I clean my teeth, and on the basin, I notice a heart shape fashioned from a single black hair. I wonder what Mummy will say when I tell her about my visitor.

I cross over the road like a biddy rather than a spring chick. Unusually, Mummy's front door is already open, and a vision of beauty with long black plaits stands in the doorway. Like Sadie, but different... It's Heather...

Mummy obviously chose my sister to keep her company during her night of sans feline. Admittedly, since Heather's offspring have reached independence, she has spent more time here with Mummy.

Even though it's freezing this morning, Heather looks like she's been for a run. She is ripped in running gear but pulls a shawl around her shoulders. I would like to say that I hope I look as good as her when I'm *her age*. I would like to say I look as good as Heather at *my age*; being considerably younger is no consolation... I wonder what Heather will say when I tell her about Sadie's visit.

'Is that Epiphany?' Mummy shouts from upstairs. I notice John sitting in his chair in the front room. I wave a hello, which he reciprocates, and then raises the newspaper to cover his face. Heather grabs me by the elbow and drags me outside.

'Are you alright?' Heather asks.

'Yes, why wouldn't I be?' I try not to breathe on her.

'It's just that Mummy saw the lights on in the pub... again... last night. I called round to see you; did that dimwit Ben forget to tell you?'

'What are you two whispering about?' Mummy cuts me off before I can answer Heather. She is prepared in finery to collect Patrice – and her question was rhetorical. 'Epiphany! Have you been drinking?'

'No! *I* haven't, but...' now is my chance to spill the beans about my exciting visitor.

'Why were the pub lights on again?' Mummy cuts me off, berating me as though I'm a teenager.

'Ah, Pippa was just telling me, she thought she heard something downstairs, thought it might have been rats,' Heather is ever the peacekeeper.

'RATS?' Mummy squeals, and I cringe.

'I didn't see anything; I just thought I heard something.'

'Oh, not this again... hearing things, seeing things, and smelling of drink in the mornings.' Mummy is one to talk, and John agrees with me by shaking his newspaper out. 'And I note that Ben's car is missing. He obviously stayed out overnight; I will not believe that he has a new job with an early start.'

'Look,' Heather gently turns Mummy around by her shoulders. 'I will drive you to the vet's.'

'But you've done so much already...' Mummy softens her tone for her firstborn, who turns to me with an expression I read as understanding and despair (of our mother). Eventually, Mummy is bundled into Heather's expensive (and environmentally friendly) car, and I can still make it to work on time in my jalopy.

Maybe Sadie is right... I am trapped. Waiting all my life for an epiphany, I've reached halfway, but I'm already there. I wipe mascara smudges from under my eyes in the ladies' at work. I wonder how old I will be when I stop wearing eyeliner and black mascara. I wonder if I'll ever stop. Then Karen bustles in looking like Mavis of Doyley Woods but sounding like Evil Edna. 'There you are!' she snips.

'Yes, I'm here... just using the facilities,' I say through my face mask.

'You've been in here ages. Your *mobile phone* keeps beeping. Mr Bland is *not happy*, AND your boyfriend has telephoned for you *again*.' Karen turns and crashes out of the room. It doesn't happen, but I imagine the door swinging back on itself and hitting me in the face. It must be the tiredness; I can't stop giggling at my presumed misfortune. The smile is soon wiped off my face when I return to my desk. A post-it note in Karen's handwriting,

a voicemail, and several text messages, they are all
communications from Ben:
  'WE NEED TO TALK.'

Chapter Six

Sadie has let herself in through the door that could not be unlocked and is surrounded by piles of my books.

'How long do you think it will take me to read all of these?' Sadie says.

'I don't know... how did you get in, Sadie? Was Ben here?' (Be still my pounding heart.)

'No, I'm afraid the lovely Ben did not let me in, I knocked, but no one answered, so I let myself in. You don't mind, do you?'

How could I possibly mind?

'What's the matter, Pippa? Have you had a really boring day at work? You should have been a librarian, like me.'

I actually thought Sadie meant she is an *actual* librarian; with all the books (my dream job). But she doesn't; she means she has been messing about. All my treasured possessions previously categorised by genre are higgledy-piggledy and not on the bookshelf.

'No... I've had an upset... I've had a message from Ben,' I flopped down on my chair.

'A message? I thought he lived here? What did it say?' Sadie looks at me from over the top of my spectacles.

'We need to talk,' my eyes fill up with tears. I had anxiously driven home in record time with a dry mouth. This obviously means Ben wants to dump me, but what if it doesn't? What if Ben actually wants to talk about something? Maybe something has happened.

'We need to talk! You know what I say to that?' Sadie challenges.

'Don't, Sadie. I know what *we need to talk* means.'

'I say fuck him.' Sadie is right, but I am anxious to know what Ben wants. Ever the optimist, I have been imagining I'm wrong, and that Ben intends to apologise for being distant... I'll forgive him... we kiss... Ben asks me to marry him, we consummate our union, and I fall pregnant with twins.

'He sent me a text last night saying he was staying over at Cassandra's... then today he needs to talk.' I feel like a teenager.

'The self-fulfilling prophecy? You did hint you thought something was going on yesterday. We just need to figure out what they're both thinking,' Sadie grips my forearms. 'Yes.'

'I can't tell what they're thinking.' (And I can't tell Sadie that I can usually read minds.)

'I mean, if Ben and Cassandra *are* having an affair... sorry. Then we should find out if Ben wants to leave you and move in with her, or is Cassandra just using him to get to you?' Sadie has taken on a project in my misery, and I like how she said 'we'.

'How can I find out? I don't know if it's true. I

might be paranoid.'

'Well, if you really want to know, there is something you can do,' Sadie takes her amulet off. 'Swing this pendulum and ask the question.'

'What?' is she mad?

'I'm only joking. That's not the real way to find out,' Sadie grins and fiddles about refastening the clasp on her chain.

'What is the real way?' she can't just leave me hanging like this.

'Look at her brain,' Sadie is deadly serious.

'What?'

'Cassandra's nostrils are so big that everyone can see her brains. Just look up her nose and you'll be able to read her thoughts.'

We both explode laughing, but I think we both know that even if we could figure out Cassandra's thoughts, it wouldn't make any difference. This is ridiculous. I need to get myself together and reply to Ben. I'm finding it so hard to resist. And I don't *want* to resist! I need to know what my boyfriend has to say (yet, it's obvious, so why should I want to put myself through it?).

'It's obvious that Ben wants to say he's leaving you, so really, you don't need to talk. Sorry,' Sadie has read my mind and blurted it out. 'There is absolutely no point meeting up with that loser. Has he taken his stuff?'

His stuff! I rush towards our bedroom... which is now *my* bedroom because Ben has taken all his things, the things he needs, essentials such as trainers, his clothes, and bedside paraphernalia. My hand is up at my face, catching my tears. It has happened. Ben has left me, and the pub hasn't even reopened yet... I turn around to rush back to my phone. Now I want to reply to all his messages. Now, I want to know what the hell is going on (even though it's obvious).

But I can't. Sadie had followed me to the bedroom with *The Big Book of Fantastic Facts*.

'Look at this book... Look at it,' Sadie is more concerned about books than my disastrous love life. To be fair, she doesn't know Ben (and she doesn't know me either, not really). She is grinning and waving a book at me...From the extensive library of escapes that my mind has enjoyed, Sadie has chosen a colouring-book-quality trivia encyclopaedia. 'What do you think?'

'It's *The Big Book of Fantastic Facts*; Aunt India gave it to me for my eleventh birthday.' Oh dear, India was Sadie's mother, not an actual aunt of mine, is Sadie annoyed at me for mentioning her? I could really do without this at the moment; my life has just dropped into my undergarments.

'I'm touched that you kept it,' Sadie hugs the telephone directory sized thing to herself. 'And that you called Mum an 'auntie'. No, I'm on about... did Mum *show* you how to read it?'

'What do you mean? It's a book. You just start at page one and keep going until you've reached the back cover.' Aunt India had no requirement to show me how to read a book at age eleven; I am convinced that I was reading at *eleven months* (although no one believed this).

'No, no, you get the book and hold it on your lap.' Sadie has stretched her legs out supine; the book is wedged between her hands. 'Close your eyes, and then let the book flop open.' Sadie completes this very manoeuvre. 'And there you have your fantastic fact of inspiration.' I pick the book up from where it lies and look at the open page. I read a story about an eighteen-month-old child who survived falling from the upper deck of a moving bus (he landed in a tree). It is not stated how this unfortunate infant fell (or if he could read, as I could at that age).

'This means nothing to me. How is that going to help me with my quandary?' I am at my wit's end. I haven't replied to Ben's messages, and he has removed any trace of himself from the flat. My earlier romantic notion is looking unlikely.

'Of course, it means nothing to *you*. You didn't do the dip!' Laughing, Sadie hops up from where she was sitting and hands me the dusty tome. 'You have to do the dip, Pippa, for it to mean anything to you.' Sadie spoke with sympathy, and in her hand, she carries a persuasive looking bottle of wine. If Sadie wasn't here, I would crumble onto the floor and lie prostate gazing at the ceiling for hours, wondering why? Why me? Why does this always happen to me? I may look like the live-action version of Crystal Tipps with my flaxen frizz, but that shouldn't mean I don't deserve love... No. Sadie is here to save me; this kind of thing would never happen to her.

Gradually, I am guided to Sadie's Thrushcross Grange. She calms me with childhood amazements and tries again to ply me with a glass of 'good for me'. I told Sadie last night, I won't be easily persuaded.

We Bible dip *The Big Book of Fantastic Facts*, and at first, it remains meaningless. Sadie is very distracting. She must have several pairs of those stretchy pants; I suppose if you find something that suits you... I wish I had that effect on clothes. I wish I had that effect on men.

'My turn! Oh... maybe not that one,' Sadie repositions herself on the rug.

'Why, what was it?'

'Oh, a mistake... It fell open on a list of monogamous mammals.'

'Great.'

'Ah! Here's one, when stick insects do *it,* they stick together for eighty days. Can you believe it? Ha! Stick together! The boy insect holds the female in place... it says 'firmly' here. He holds her firmly... Gross.'

Is Sadie trying to tell me that things could be worse? I could be a stick insect? I take the book of fruitless facts from her, as it is my go. I close my eyes, and the book drops open.

'A bearded woman? Does this mean I keep getting dumped because I've got facial hair?' I haven't (I touch my chin to check).

'No, but you're getting warmer,' Sadie's cheeks are getting warmer. The heat from her wine-drinking radiates, and I confess I am feeling better too.

'Here's one about a vicar who skied at the same time as performing a church service to raise money for charity. Aww, that sounds lovely.'

'Hmmm, religion,' Sadie shakes her head seriously at this silly situation. 'Have another go; it's on me.'

'You're deadly serious, aren't you?' I take in Sadie's nod. 'OK, a circus act. It's a man who can walk on bottles.'

'What kind of bottles?'

'Prosecco, champagne, gin... mostly alcohol.' What has this got to do with anything? (Although, I admit to taking in all the facts and figures of this story.)

'That's it! Your special power!'

'What?'

'You are being guided to your special power. This is how you will resolve your... thing with Ben. What can you do that no one else can?' Sadie is ecstatic. 'You know, if you were a super-hero, what would your power be?'

'Not smashing empty wine bottles in my late thirties.' I scan my mind. I don't know what my superpower is. I bet that if *anyone* was asked the same question, they would be stumped. I think about revealing that I have memories of reading as an infant. But I have something better up my sleeve.

'I can tell what people think of me without them saying anything.' I folded my arms in triumph, and the glamorous bottle walker folds back into the book.

'What?' Sadie looks deflated.

'Yes, it's like I can read minds. Sometimes, what people say is the opposite of what they think. Even if their body language says one thing, I can tell what they're really thinking. Like Ben and Cassandra, I knew what was going on without *really* knowing.' I have never spoken of this before. I suppose I've always been frightened of appearing paranoid, worrying too much about what people think or at the least overthinking things.

'Everyone can do that, Pippa,' Sadie has this knack for making me feel better but daft at the same time, so challenging Sadie makes me tingle. It's not like nonchalantly strolling into work late with a little speech prepared for my non-boss Karen. 'Well, go on then... what's your superpower?'

'I don't have magical powers! What do you think I am?' Sadie claps her mother's book shut, and we both cough dusty coughs.

Chapter Seven

The last thing I remember about yesterday is asking Sadie if she is in a relationship. She didn't answer, and I couldn't tell what she was thinking.

Sadie left me with the overwhelming feeling of letting go, a powerful tool to weld the chink in my armour. I'm not sure if it was the distraction of India's cheap grimoire or Sadie's unconditional empathy, but I managed to resist texting Ben or re-following Cassandra. Insomnia and Wi-Fi provide mischief to the scorned, but now that I have left it twenty-four hours, I'm sure I can carry on.

I can't use my mobile phone while I'm driving anyway, can I? Where even is Ben, though? He's obviously not arsed about me. I wonder if he wanted to talk about how he was involved in a weird accident, or he's had to go into hospital for some reason. I wonder when I'm going to stop seeing the best in everyone.

I arrive early at work. Karen notices me pull up into one of the parking spaces, pretends she hasn't seen me, and power walks through the entrance door. The tattoo place downstairs is already open; it usually doesn't until ten o'clock. Is this my chance to book a tarot card reading? It's like I am drawn to divination all of a sudden. Everywhere I look, the universe is commanding me to get my cards read. Not only have the sign in the shop underneath my office, but a teabag burst in my cup, making me wish I could read leaves. Then the film version of the book I just read by Joanne Harris came on television the other day. And speaking of television, when I switched it on for company at bedtime, a woman on a reality show had her tarot cards read. Somebody is trying to tell me something.

Karen completely ignored me when I walked past her desk. I did enquire downstairs, but the fortune teller is off sick because her son's school has a case of Covid (shame she didn't see that coming). So much for the universe trying to tell me something; this must mean that the 'thing' has already happened. Ben has left me, and I didn't see it coming.

Mr Bland has asked to see me. I don't like today already, and it's only half-past ten.

'Ah, come in, Phillipa,' Mr Bland gets my name wrong. He has a solid Yorkshire accent. I've tried my best to avoid contact with my boss since he called me on the internal line and asked me to 'go fetch ma coooooat, luv,' which he had left in the Wetherspoons across the road from our office. Thankfully, the reason he couldn't collect this himself was that he had a lengthy meeting. Unfortunately, Karen noticed that I had wandered around the town for hours trying to figure out what Mr Bland meant... My internal phone line has been broken ever since. I decide not to correct Mr Bland about my name. He could be giving me the sack, so I'd prefer to get this over and done with quickly (and explaining how 'Pippa' is short for 'Epiphany' has taken up far too much of my life already).

'Well, sit tha down then,' Mr Bland stands from his desk to offer me a chair, but I take it before he can move around his desk. He sounds friendly, which is weird considering I'm about to be re-united with my P45. 'Karen came in to see me this morning.'

Of course, she did.

'Don't look so worried; it's nothing like that.'

Does Mr Bland have the same superpower as me?

'I asked Karen t'check everyone's annual leave and time owing from work. Seems it all got a bit out of flunter because of everything,' Mr Bland smoothes down his tie.

'Everything?' I say.

'You know, working from home during the lockdown. Most people used up their holidays and such like because of childcare and so on. O'course, no one could go on holiday. So, it seems you've accrued some leave.'

'What? I mean, pardon?'

'You didn't take any holidays last year and haven't made a dent in this year. So, I'm asking you to take two weeks' leave starting from... now if you like.'

'What?' I mean, I am half prepared to go home (to my empty flat), but this is the opposite of what I'm expecting.

'Yes, take a holiday. A staycation they're calling it on the news. I don't want to get sued, you see.' Mr Bland tries to end our meeting by messing about with his day-planner.

'Sued?'

'The wife's sister works at the hospital. There are all sorts of grievances goin' in over substantive posts being messed about wi'...'

'Oh,' I have no idea what Mr Bland is talking about, but I don't want to spend the rest of the day wandering around the town.

Karen holds my coat open for me when I leave Mr Bland's office. I've never seen her smile before. 'Have a good rest, Pippa. You need... you deserve it.' If I hadn't turned around at that moment, I am sure that Karen would have kissed me on the cheek.

Two weeks' freedom? I hope Sadie visits again.

I should be thinking about all the things I could do during my leave as I drive home. Instead, I am wondering how I can pull my car into The Peacock's car park without Mummy noticing. This may sound selfish, but I think I deserve a bit of time to myself instead of ferrying Patrice to her unnecessary vet appointments. And I haven't told Mummy about Ben's disappearance or Sadie's appearance.

I open my front door, and my senses are met by the smell of sweet popcorn and burnt kernels. This can't be Ben returning and begging to be allowed back. Aside from his car not being outside, he would *never* burn the popcorn. It's one of the few things he was good at. We would regularly have film nights in the flat during lockdown. Although I never got to choose the film, I did enjoy snuggling with my feet up eating goodies.

'Pippa!' Sadie sits in the big chair cross-legged with a large bowl of popcorn in her lap. She is wearing those leggings again, and my mind switches to the pairs and pairs of them I have tried. I'm a sucker for anything advertised as shapewear. I wonder how Sadie got in.

'Did you happen to see Mummy's car over the road?' I've no idea why this was the first thing I asked. I was expecting my flat to be utterly bereft at this weird time that I'm not usually here.

'No. No, I haven't seen your mum. I just heard the commotion,' Sadie points towards Mummy's house.

'What commotion?'

'She was tearing a strip off the builders,' Sadie smirks.

'Well, that's nothing new.'

'Something about keys,' Sadie looks as though she is trying to remember. She must have excellent hearing.

'The key thing is nothing new. Mummy is always having the locks changed.' I sit down, and Sadie hurriedly tidies the cluttered coffee table.

'I've been watching *When Harry Met Sally*. It's not for you.'

'I love that film! I do, I love that film, and I haven't seen it for ages.'

'No. It's about a couple who split up, and then they get back together again. You'll just relate that to you and Ben. You're not allowed to watch it,' Sadie points the remote at the television, decidedly pressing its buttons.

'No, it isn't! It's about a man and woman who hate one another at first, then they become friends, but they don't realise they are falling in love.'

'Well... I don't want you relating it to *anything*... I've decided you can't watch it. You can't watch anything. You've been sent home from work, haven't you?'

'How did you know?' I have so many questions for Sadie.

'You set off for work this morning, and you've arrived back before midday, so I worked it out.'

I didn't know that Sadie was still here when I left for work. Has she moved in without me realising?

'I didn't take any annual leave last year, so they've made me take two weeks' holiday. I was going to get my tarot cards read, but the clairvoyant is off because her son has been sent home from school. She didn't see that coming!' I repeat my own joke for Sadie, but she bats me away.

'You don't need your fortune told, Pippa. You already know what's happening. And you don't need to watch any films either.'

'But... when I smelt the popcorn, it made me want to watch something... Ben would never let me choose the film.'

'See. This is what I mean. You're relating everything to Ben, aren't you? Popcorn, films, and everything; you need to get over him as quickly as possible. Now, I've been looking at romantic comedies for you all morning to research what you should do,' Sadie is deadly serious. This is kind of annoying; I know what to do because I've done it before. 'You shouldn't do what you usually do after a breakup.'

'Well, I haven't contacted him,' I defensively snatch the popcorn from Sadie and start chewing.

'I know, I know,' Sadie soothes. 'If you read anything, let it be an Agatha Christie.'

'What?' Sadie sounds nuts, like a sister, but nuts.

'Yes, Agatha Christie; Hercule Poirot is the furthest thing from a breakup with Ben. I've even made you a pile; this one is a Miss Marple, but that's fine. She was a spinster. Do not relate that to yourself, Pippa. You're too young to be a spinster.'

'Alright,' I take the books from Sadie. I didn't realise that I own so many murder mysteries. 'I hope you're right, Sadie. Even the word spinster sounds grim and archaic.'

'Yes, karma's a bitch, isn't it?'

'Pardon?' what does she mean? I haven't done anything wrong.

'Cassandra's a bitch.' Sadie is still sorting through my books. I must have misheard her.

Chapter Eight

I couldn't describe what happened during the afternoon. Sadie was correct to ban film-watching because I have spent far too much time in this flat. The Peacock is empty yet still tempting. Instead, Sadie is Shug Avery to my Celie teaching me how to wear pants and do my hair. The rest can only be told as magic, I walked down those stairs looking like Madame Bovary. It is early evening now, and Sadie and I sit in a garden that does not belong to Mummy's pub. I'm wearing a pair of shiny black leggings, which so far have failed to damage my pride. My flaxen hair is folded and folded again, framing my face with voluminous waves. My fair complexion is mirrored in Sadie's aviators.

A carefree attitude has gripped the gathered crowd. We are British, and this is the freedom we have craved. Sadie sip, sips, and sips as we indulge in some powerful people watching. We attract casual and cursory glances, which I am confident will continue to second looks as the night draws on.

The waiting staff appeared bemused at our drinks order. Sadie told them that asking for a double would 'save them returning to our table again.' This feels awesome. I have never before so successfully squeezed into shiny stretchy pants, and I am on fire. I am also great company; Sadie is laughing her arse off at everything I say. Let the good times roll; this is far superior to popcorn and chick flicks, finer than film night with boring Ben. Speaking of...

'Oh my God. I don't believe it,' Sadie loudly greets the incoming Ben and Cassandra. What a coincidence they should be in the same pub garden as us. They do not look happy. I suppose it is better to see them now, rather than months and years of anxiety that I may bump into either of them. Ben looks as though he has received a Cassandra make-over during the seventy-two hours (or however long it is) since I last saw him. Cassandra whispers something to Ben, which I catch as 'making a fool of herself again.' Sadie and I continue sipping, and although we started off shivering outside, faux fur and other tonics have warmed us. All my life, Heather instilled in me that ginger is potent, and now I know that she was right. I also now know that Ben definitely *is* with Cassandra. There is no getting away from it; this is the way we get revenge on a cold and windy evening.

Half an hour passes, and I am unable to be-cause neurosis roots me to the spot, but Sadie releases her long legs from the picnic bench. She struts her heeled biker boots over to the unhappy couple. Am I about to discover what Sadie's super-power is?

'Hello Benito,' Sadie makes sure everyone can hear her (the crowd certainly are all looking at her).

'Look, I'm sorry, OK, I shouldn't have left like that.' Ben ignores Sadie's attempt to Italianize his name and ignores my need for an apology or explanation by passing it on to my half-sister's half-sister.

I am overwhelmed with gratification. Sadie has stood up to confront Ben and Cassandra on my behalf. I decide to rejoice by grabbing one of the waiters and order a bottle of champagne.

'After everything you've done,' Cassandra dismisses Sadie by shaking her head. What on earth does she mean? Sadie hasn't done anything, or has she?

'Look, we've just come out to grab something to eat while we can,' Ben is nervous and awkward. I am enjoying this (I regret leaving the popcorn at home).

'While you can? Do you mean until Tristan returns?'

Tristan is Cassandra's husband. He always smelt of musk, and I'm not a fan of hearing his name. I remember him chatting me up (even though Tristan is Cassandra's husband). He gave me two options; did I want to go Ceroc dancing or for a cheeky Chinese takeaway? I giggled and asked him if he only goes on dates beginning with 'C'. That was some time ago.

'You have got some nerve,' Cassandra's eyes dart around for a member of the waiting staff. And one duly attends the damsel's rescue.

'Sorry, Miss, we're asking everyone to remain seated. It's waiter service only at the moment.'

Then Sadie did something. She turned to me and picked up my recently delivered bottle of champagne, which was neatly nestled in an ice bucket. She quietly placed the costly sine qua non of ice buckets on the outdoor table in front of Ben and Cassandra, whispered 'enjoy', turned, and walked away. Sadie added her glamour by taking in both of them staring at her behind.

I continued with my invisibility, inhaling a ginger mixer. I can hear Cassandra whispering loudly to the babysitter on her phone. I can't help staring over, and she uses her middle finger to slide her sunglasses back into position. I hope the plastic smudges her eyebrow pencil to make her look like a surprised clown. That's funny, I laugh. I'm laughing to myself, I haven't shared the joke with Sadie, but she is laughing too.

We laugh long and loud until tears almost blind us. Then Ben and Cassandra drain their glasses and leave (not without bagging my gift of champagne).

'Cheers!' I salute.

Chapter Nine

It will only be a matter of time until Mummy discovers my compulsory absence from the workplace. I decided to beat her to it by knocking on her door bright and early. I also need to face the music about Ben's departure; I know Mummy will have noticed this (and have plenty to say about it). Things happen in threes, and I have three things to say to Jacquetta.

As I breathe in the smell of cedar and buttercups, I know that today will be a good day. The sun sparkles up the tarmac between The Peacock and Mummy's house like a moat. I have already tackled the drawbridge when I see John fiddling with the massive bunch of keys required to unlock the fortress. Mummy has a front door, a screen, and a porch that separate her from the outside world. The moat I mentioned was imaginary. I see Mummy pushing John out of the way through the bi-fold Venetian.

'Epiphany!' Mummy shrieks. She always seems surprised to see me, even though I live over the road.

Can I smell booze?

I follow Mummy's floating happi coat into her parlour. She may own a pub, but she's fancy.

'Oh, Patrice!' Mummy's cat has a new lease of

life. She bounds onto my lap as though I'm a long, lost owner. Cats always like me. I must get one now that Ben has completed his inevitable flit. I must also remember to ask future potentials if they enjoy felines. Got to like a C A T if you wanna be with me... Goodness, I'm in a good mood!

'Cats always like you, Epiphany. I can't understand it...' Mummy shakes her head.

'What's not to like?' John leaps to my rescue.

'Thank you, John. I am adorable,' I say.

John laughs unsurely.

'No, I mean, I can't understand why Patrice is so full of beans. One minute she's forcing me to the vet's again with her moaning big eyes. The next, she leaps around with no sign of rhinitis,' Mummy pets and fusses Patrice. Anyone would think Mummy prefers her cats to adopt the sick role.

'Did they give her steroids at the vet's? That will explain her ten men dance,' John has a point.

'Perhaps Patrice is PREGNANT!' Mummy completely ignores John. 'Oh, you *must* adopt, Pippa, if she is with kitten.'

'Maybe I will, I can now.' I have been here almost half an hour, and there has been no mention of why I am not at work or that Ben's car has permanently disappeared from the car park. Maybe I could get away with discussing neither?

'Only time will tell, won't it, Patrice?' Mummy tickles the cat's belly and disappears under the pretence of making coffee. She has a machine for that.

I have already provided one prompt; I *can* get a cat now because Ben (who doesn't like cats) is gone. Better to get it over with and spill the beans because sitting in silence with John is pointless. 'I can adopt one of the kittens... if they exist... because Ben has left me.' There. I've blurted it out in record time; perhaps John shall mention it to Mummy later that I am single again. Instead, he says something I'm not expecting.

'You know, I'm not sure you're allowed pets on your lease.' John appears deep in thought, as though he is trying to remember.

'What?' what lease?

'You can't have cats or pets in the flat, Epiphany,' Mummy agrees with John and pretends he hasn't spoken at the same time. I like her style.

'What do you mean? It's your pub!' I have lived in the flat above The Peacock for as long as I can remember. It was not long after Mummy married John. He ran the place at the time, and Mummy was a silent partner. She would silently indulge in a nip of 'invisible' (gin or vodka) and occasionally collect the odd finished glass or two. I think Oswald was around at the time, but heaven knows what part he played in the running of things. My father, Maddox, managed The Peacock before Oswald. With regards to Mummy's affections, Oswald came before Maddox.

I was about seventeen when I left home and

made the short journey across the road, and I've been here ever since. Over twenty years later, I don't remember any details. This is Mummy's pub, so I've just presumed that I'm still living at home (but across the road).

'I'm sure the others will... Not to worry,' Mummy bats my question away as she has just remembered she has one of her own. 'Aren't you supposed to be in the office?'

'They said on the news that the pandemic isn't over, so she's probably had to work from home again.' John talks about me as though I'm not there. I don't mind; Mummy is about to ignore him.

'I hope you haven't been sent home again? You know I had to hold Mr Bland in a state of transfixion to get you that job,' Mummy tuts.

Honestly, something happens *one time*, and Jacquetta thinks it will happen *every time*. She is convinced that men are magnetised to her. In the case of my boss, Mummy indeed enquired about positions available, but I have held my place at that firm by my own capabilities. As Sadie would say, I can 'do sums'. Speaking of... two down one to go... I am yet to spill the beans about my exciting visitor.

'I'm on annual leave,' I answered Mummy, and she gave me one of her *whatever next* looks.

'You're on holiday?' Now even John doesn't believe me.

'Yes, annual leave. Mr Bland doesn't want to get sued.' If everything I say sounds like a lie, maybe I should hold off telling Mummy about Sadie.

'He never struck me as the litigious type,' Mummy looks at John for approval of her assumption.

'Well, that's why I'm at home. I needed the time off.'

'Oh! I knew it. Epiphany, what have you done now?'

'No, not that way. Mr Bland called me into the office...' I explain but being called into the office will provide Mummy ammunition.

'Sounds fishy to me, Epiphany; it reminds me of the time when...' Mummy's recollection is halted by my sister's arrival. 'Heather!' Jacquetta is always thrilled to see her firstborn. Always.

'Hello, Pippa, what are you doing here?'

'She's been sent home from work again, but I'm sure it's nothing your mother can't sort out.' John talks about me (again).

'Oh, darling. Are you alright?' Heather may sound caring yet, she was the most condescending during my last spell of enforced absence.

'I'm...' I cough. I want to say I'm fine, thank you, but I start coughing. I start coughing, and I can't stop. It's as though my throat is filled with the same tickling sensation I was plagued with as a child.

Chapter Ten

No doubt Heather would have been filled in about my holiday at home. And if John can stop watching the news for once, the cat will be out of the bag about Ben and me separating.

Today was meant to be a good day, but now I can see Heather walking across my imagined moat.

I miss Sadie.

'Sweetie, are you alright?' Heather has let herself in via the door (the same one that Mummy has trouble opening).

'In here,' I answer Heather without answering her.

'I'd love a cup of tea if you're making one.'

I wasn't, but I am in the kitchen, mainly to look out of the window onto the road below. I usually have to stay here a while until I have spotted a second magpie.

'So, how are you?' I ask Heather. I never quite know what to talk about with my sister.

'No! How are you? I never did like that freeloader, and I'm glad he's dumped you.'

'Thanks?' I answer Heather with a question.

'I'm not glad for you, obviously. Breaking up

is hard to do, Pippa. It happens to the best of us, even me.' Heather helps herself to two mugs from my cupboard and gazes longingly at the kettle. It seems Mummy's bitter coffee has not quenched her thirst.

'When have you ever been dumped by anyone? Rhys hasn't left you, has he?'

'Don't be silly! Rhys will never leave me!' Heather laughs. 'I meant this is something that most women go through. You'll be fine. Leaving you for that hideous creature Cassandra must hurt, though.'

'Yes, it does,' I sigh and squeeze the teabags. 'Hang on, I didn't tell John that bit.'

'What's John got to do with anything? I saw it on Facey.'

Oh no, this is most horrendous. John did not repeat my sad news to Heather; my misfortune was spread across social media like thick-cut marmalade. Mummy has failed to notice Ben's absence from my life (which means she has not seen Sadie coming and going either). I must check.

'Has Mummy seen Cassandra's Facebook post?'

'No, Jacquetta doesn't do social media, you know that. Cassandra's horribly gloating about her houseguest, though. I thought she was still married to Tristan? Still, she is rather attractive, despite her family.' Heather smells of lavender today.

'Her forehead is too big,' I will not have it that Cassandra is good looking. Not with those nostrils.

'I suppose, but she is very slim. Does Ben prefer that sort of thing?' Heather puffs her cheeks out and then makes a raspberry sound with her lips. Why must my sister torment me so?

'Here's your tea.' It's a shame that I hadn't asked Heather to sit in the lounge; I would have spat in it while she wasn't looking.

'Thanks, I'm serious, Pippa. You need to be careful going out on your own to spy on your forsaker.' Heather burns her mouth on the tea and reaches for a biscuit. The thing is, since falling out of favour with Cassandra, I have few friends. It is difficult to get close to anyone because of my psychic affliction. Meetings with friends would always end with the question; *you're not leaving already, are you?* I couldn't exactly say *yes, because I have read your mind, and you slagged me off in your head.* Anyway, I wasn't on my own when I bumped into Ben and Cassandra. I was with my half-sister's half-sister. I must tell Heather about Sadie, but I can't get a word in.

'I'm glad in a way that you've fallen out with Cassandra. When you were little, you had this awful habit of pretending to be other people, and you used to copy her like she was the Queen of Sheba. You wanted to look like Daddy's wife too. Just be yourself, *Epiphany*.'

'Because everyone else is taken...' I quote Oscar Wilde to Heather, but she didn't notice. I noticed what she said, though; Cassandra had nothing to do with India. Sadie was her daughter.

Heather is eating all my biscuits.

'Jacquetta tells me you were sent home from work again,' Heather is allowed to call Mummy by her Christian name. I think this was from the time when Jacquetta used to pretend that Heather was her sister.

'Again?' I roll my eyes. 'I am on holiday! Mr Bland doesn't want to get sued.' My two weeks' leave is getting wasted on repeating myself (I miss Sadie).

'And this coincides with Ben dumping you? Rotten luck, Pipsqueak.'

'PippA, Heather. I'm called Pippa.'

'Your name is Epiphany,' Heather sips her tea.

'Any more of that, and I shall have to start calling you Hazel again.' That should teach her.

'Oww, don't be like that; I've come to tell you I'm going to do something nice for you, PippA.'

Oh, joy. What could Heather possibly do for me?

'I'm taking you to a women's healing retreat.'

There it is. Hippy shit.

'Can't I just read an Agatha Christie?' I know Heather will ignore this.

'I know what you're thinking, but this is to save you from Jacquetta. She wants to take you on a non-alcoholic afternoon tea at the cafe in the middle of the nature reserve. So, I have stepped up and offered to cure you with breathing techniques and ecstatic dancing.'

Enforced dancing. Great.

'You're welcome,' Heather prompts a thank you from me, but the tickling sensation is back in my throat. 'Oh, you're not coming down with something, are you? Rotten luck if you're on leave from work, you should have taken a sickie.'

'No, don't worry, I don't have Covid.'

'I don't believe in it, Pipsqueak. It's all a conspiracy.'

And Mummy thinks I'm the mental one.

'She's still married.' I have to change the subject. Since Rhys and Heather got rid of their television, they have become alternate reality enthusiasts.

'Who? What?' Heather has forgotten what she came here to upset me with.

'Tristan and Cassandra. They're still married.'

'Ah, but he's away at the moment, isn't he?' Heather stuffs another ginger nut in her mouth.

'Yes, I don't know how long for though.'

'Don't you?' Heather asks as though she thinks I know the answer. I often get into these paranoiac confabs with my older sister. She knows that I know, and I know that she knows I know, or something.

Chapter Eleven

Despite my sister's intervention, Jacquetta has arranged to take me to the cafe in the middle of the nature reserve for non-alcoholic afternoon tea.

'The tradition of afternoon tea has been bastardised in recent years, I believe. Actual tea is swapped for Italian sparkling wine.' This is Jacquetta; she drinks, and she thinks she knows things. And yes, I am allowed to refer to Mummy by her Christian name because Heather has joined us.

'I read somewhere that gin was drunk from teacups during the prohibition period in America.' And this is Heather, the turncoat. I thought she was supposed to be saving me with menopause yoga?

'Filth,' Jacquetta does not like it when Americans change things. 'The word 'teacups' has a 'u' in it, though how did they cope?'

'What?' I say. Mummy sounds bonkers, but Heather laughs.

'Good one Jacquetta, or should I say Mom?' Heather puts on a voice, and Mummy clinks her teacup in celebration of their imperialism.

'Well, it doesn't bother me. I don't drink, as you know,' I really could do with a drink right now (despite my allergy).

'Oh, you're so funny, Pippa. We three are on fire today!' Heather professes a comic quality today.

'Now Epiphany, I did not bring you up to be a liar,' Mummy takes on a stern tone.

'I don't lie, what would I be lying about?' what *would* I be lying about? I don't drink.

I remember the last time I went out for a non-alcoholic afternoon tea with Mummy. It was before the pandemic, and we met up in a place that was not in the middle of a nature reserve. I think Mummy took me along to deflect her 'friend's' personality. The friend (I forget her name) juggled work, looking after the family, and running her home. Not to mention keeping a husband. The poor thing was struggling with the trappings of the modern working woman, *and* she had an hour's commute to work either way. Mummy told the friend not to worry because she could see that something would change for her very soon. The woman seemed very pleased. Mummy told me later that she wouldn't be seeing her 'friend' again because she didn't tip. I wonder if Mummy realises how strong her powers of persuasion are because the 'friend' no longer suffers the long commute (she works from home since the lockdown). I can hear Mummy talking to Heather about her in the background.

'She wants to see me again because she has

another problem. Now that her work-life balance is restored, her husband has left her.' Jacquetta and Heather turned to look at me with exactly the same expression.

'Speaking of...' Mummy says.

'It is Splitsville City around here all of a sudden,' Heather enhances her look of pity. The divorce scenario would never happen to her. Heather is Hera with hazel eyes brightening against her peacock dress.

'Well, I am feeling fine about the whole thing,' I can also feel a tickle in my throat.

'We love you, Epiphany,' Mummy says.

Especially when you have an audience, Mother.

'And we care about you,' Heather echoes.

'But it hurts us to see you going down the same road as *last time*.'

Even though I drifted off, I heard those words *like last time* rolling around the middle of the nature reserve like a weasel, cunningly good and bad luck at the same time. I admit that Tristan's infatuation with me was unfortunate because he is Cassandra's husband. But it really wasn't my fault. None of this is my fault, and in any case, *last time* was a long time ago. *This time* I have a new sister; Sadie has given me the gift of emancipation. To be free from my current heartbreak, all I have to do is reread a few Agatha Christie's. I am unable to explain this to Jacquetta and Heather. Aside from the unrelenting coughs, I can't get a word in.

'We remember what happened with Tristan,' Mummy says. How can she remember something she didn't know about at the time?

'You do get fascinated with people, Pippa. I know this has been rotten luck for you that Cassandra has now stolen your boyfriend after what happened…'

'Are you telling us the absolute truth about being sent on holiday? Because the past few days have been very reminiscent of what happened *last time*, Epiphany.'

'Tell the truth, little sister; have you been suspended from work again?'

'We didn't like Ben though, did we, Heather?'

'We didn't like Ben *for you*,' Heather rounds things off as though she and Jacquetta are one entity. I can't stop coughing, and people are looking over. Mummy and Heather are face mask avoiders, but this went largely unnoticed until things started opening up again. I literally pull my pullover over the bottom of my face. With streaming eyes, I turn away from my mother and sister and scurry out of the building. They will obviously presume I am fleeing their intervention, but I am sparing the gathered ladies of leisure from germaphobia. Sitting two metres apart is not enough for a coughing fit in an enclosed space. None of this is my fault.

After I composed myself, I decide to drive

home alone in my jalopy. There is plenty of room in Heather's environmentally friendly wagon for Mummy. I've had quite enough of the pair of them, this is my holiday, and I shall spend it how I choose (and this doesn't involve raking over the past). I haven't been allowed to explain what happened with Tristan because Mummy and Heather do not listen. It wasn't my fault, and I don't know why they are punishing me by bringing it up now all this time later. Jacquetta will no doubt persuade Heather to take her to the nearest pub (that she doesn't own) to order a 'gin and tonic, *proper* gin, *proper* tonic. Hold the garnish, but not the ice.' Mummy is such a lush; she has her drinks order prepared for any occasion. She is a hypocrite. Although to be fair, Mummy and Heather hardly touched on the subject of my sobriety. I feel no guilt for Heather's non-drinking-drive home. She was the one who insisted on moving up to Pendle. I saw her eying up my original features the other day. It's *my* flat, and she can't have it.

Chapter Twelve

I have not managed to turn my mind off, and I am getting no rest during the fortnight's leave I have taken without my consent. I know I am asleep because I am having a dream about attending my hairdresser's birthday party. I know this is a dream because I haven't been to the hairdressers recently (not even since everything reopened). Also, Heather is here, and I don't wish to speak to Heather at the moment, so I must be asleep. Heather is such a busybody that I am distracted enough to park in the wrong space at the front of the building. I sit here alone, sipping a glass of lime and soda water (because dream-me has forgotten my purse). Then the smell of apples, mint, and cloves fills my senses, and something brushes my foot.

I know this is real because Sadie doesn't know my hairdresser.

'Morning sunshine, the earth says hello,' Sadie stands at the side of my bed, wearing those same black shiny leggings and a grin.

'Hello,' I rub my eyes and think about going to the bathroom. I can't speak to Sadie until I have brushed my teeth and used the facilities, yet I don't find her wake-up call intrusive. Sadie follows me, and she doesn't care when I don't close the bathroom door – like a sister wouldn't mind.

Then I hear it. I hear it before I see her and the soft, sweet baby meows swell my heart. Sadie steps to the side to reveal a cardboard box with holes pushed in the top.

'I found you a cat, a kitten. She's here in the box, Pippa. She found you, Pippa,' Sadie bends to open the makeshift kitty carrier. Her dark hair meets the cardboard, and she reaches in, collecting the tiniest cat I have ever seen in my life. The cat looks straight at me with blind kitten eyes and meows opening her mouth like a folded fortune teller. I think I love her. Sadie passes the kitten to me; she is soft and spiky at the same time. She smells of love, and her little pink tongue reaches for the sunshine. This cat is mine.

'Is this another strategy to cure me of heartbreak?' I ask Sadie. Even in my hands, the kitten tries to rub itself up against me. 'Because if it is, she has worked, and is much better than Jacquetta and Heather's attempts at tyranny.' I kiss the kitten's head.

'She found you; she wants to be with you, Pippa.' Sadie reassures me, without having to ask about Mummy and Heather's lecture. She unpacks the kitten's belongings of a bowl, blanket, and kitten food.

'What shall we name her?' I say.

For the first time since our reunion, I see a side to Sadie that I haven't seen since swim class. She turned on her heeled biker boot and stares me right in the eyes. Her irises are two disarming discs of practically all hazel. For a few seconds, we stare at one another. This was not like the gazing admiration of Sadie's blouson on the day she returned. This is a quagmire.

'I think this cat will be named India, after my mother.'

Shit. India's death is the one thing I have managed to avoid talking to Sadie about. Obviously, I'm full of condolence for her. They were so close, and to lose your mother so young and in such a violently shocking and tragic way.

'It's a lovely name, for a... could India be a cat's name?' I have not broken eye contact with Sadie because I am unable to.

'I think so, Pippa,' Sadie smiles, but her eyes are still locked on mine. She handles the kitten again, freeing me of the needling. 'That way, Patrice can stay alive.'

'What? I mean, pardon?' What is Sadie going on about? She has filled my flat with tension, and now it seems she is about to admit to theriocide.

'It's a superstition, isn't it?'

'No,' I say. Sadie is making things up now.

'It is. Everyone knows it,' Sadie turns away from me. She can't possibly expect me to believe a superstition exists about naming a kitten after the person whose death you caused in a vain attempt to save another cat's life. 'It's the one about when one kitten is born, another cat has to die.'

I feel the tickling sensation trying to close my throat. 'What about the St. Ives riddle? Each sack had seven cats, and each cat had seven kits.' I try to give Sadie the defensive yet triumphant look I learnt in the playground, but it's no good. I look like a pickpocket with chewing gum under their fingernails.

'Kits, cats, sacks, and wives, how many were going to St. Ives?' Sadie bursts out laughing and bundles India Kitten back into my arms. 'Your face! You are so easy to wind up. What do you think I am? Some sort of cat hippy? You're getting me mixed up with our sister-in-common. She's the one with all the furry familiars.'

I laugh too because it is funny. It's as laughable as a bang on your window on a winter's night that turns out to be someone you're expecting. My own stupid fear amuses me. There is no need to admit to Sadie that I killed India; it wasn't my fault, and I didn't land the final blow.

We snuggle with my secret in the living room. We drink coffee and eat biscuits. India Kitten entertains us by chasing after crumbs and dusting them with her whiskers. I suppose we all have different ways of dealing with bereavement. I believe we all have different ways of coping with guilt (I'm drowning in mine). It must have been hard for Sadie at the time, but now she appears as relaxed as she was at swim class about her mother's death. I admit I have blocked out any memories of my tragically haunted past. I have done such a good job of forgetting that I cannot remember. No one knows the truth about what happened that night, not even me. I think Jacquetta and Heather suspect, and I know that's why they keep me on a tight leash.

'I was so sorry about your mum,' I say, and I really mean it. I have managed to talk about India without mentioning the day she died. Sadie is not so gentle.

'It was partly her fault. She only had one eye, didn't she?' Sadie draws a circle with her finger around the kitten's left eye. 'Mum went out that night dressed all in black and walked along the road with no care for her own safety,' Sadie throws her head back and smiles at the ceiling.

I sort of make a catch-in-my throat noise between a nervous laugh and a gasp. As much as I love Sadie, it is hard to know how to take her making light of her mother's death. Yet who am I to judge? Who knows how I will cope when Jacquetta dies? (if she ever does; I often wonder if she is immortal).

'She only had herself to blame, Pippa. Everyone knows the drill; if you must go walking into the night to warn your niece about a bad love match, always wear a high-vis. Always.'

Shit.

'I didn't know Aunt India had a niece,' I say in a small voice.

Sadie turns to me, nods her head slightly, and

raises her eyebrows. 'Especially if you only have one eye,' Sadie concludes. Did that nod mean me? Does she know after all? India was not my auntie; she was Mummy's ex-husband's new lover. And India was Sadie's mother. I was not India's niece (although I did call her auntie the other day and Sadie seemed to like it). I feel light-headed.

'Does this coffee have something in it?' I panic; it is only half-past ten.

'You like it virgin,' Sadie shakes her head.

'Virgin! Where do you think you are? This is an impromptu coffee morning, not a bourbon binge.'

'Shhh!' Sadie presses her finger to her lips. 'India's sleeping.'

We both look at the kitten curled up in her blanket. We both eat another biscuit. The dark patch on India Kitten's left eye will darken as she grows. She did choose me; she is India Kitten.

'How did your mum get her... why did she...?' How does one ask the question, *what was the eye patch about?*

'Why did she only have one eye? That's what you want to ask, isn't it?' Sadie is a mind reader (like me).

'Well,' I venture.

'She caught a zip in the eye at a heavy metal festival.' Sadie is so matter of fact. 'It's true, Pippa. The singer... I forget which band... asked the crowd to take their coats and swing them around their heads.'

There is my nervous gasping noise again.

'Most of the audience suffered the smell of body odour, but Mum copped for the zip of someone's hoodie in her left eye.'

'Oh shit! That's awful,' I say.

'It must have been, for Mum,' Sadie picks up India Kitten. I read that you must never disturb a sleeping cat, but it doesn't seem to mind.

'I don't know what to say,' I don't. I literally don't know what to say. I spend a lot of time vexed with Mummy and Heather because I can't get a word in. Now when I get my chance, I'm silent.

'You don't have to say anything, Pippa. It was a long time ago, happened before I was born, it was no big deal. You must agree that Mum styled out her eye patch, and it's only like wearing a face mask.'

'Ha, yes, you're right,' I agree with Sadie's sentiment (apart from her mother's rhinestone Jolly Roger that came out on Halloween).

'This is the way we cover our eye, isn't it India?' Sadie kisses the kitten. 'You know, what else feels a long time ago? It feels a long time ago that Mum died.'

'I know,' I say and put my head against Sadie's head. She seems oblivious to my involvement, the night I ruined everyone's life. Still, whenever I ask Sadie a question about herself, she changes the subject, doesn't answer, or disappears. And that's the way I like it... I'm *such* a people pleaser.

'Right! Let's not waste your holiday petting this attention seeker,' Sadie means the kitten.

'I'm not! I love today!'

'Pippa! You are one hot chocolate away from a chick flick. Get your feet off the pouffe, and let's have a makeover day. You do me, and I'll do you.' Sadie runs her fingers through her long, shiny, dark hair. She does not need a makeover.

Soon we are into the second half of the day; the sun has passed noon. Daylight will not last for many more hours but stretches in generosity day by day. No doubt Heather will be trying to bore me with her sunflower seedling selfies soon; I won't respond until I've had an apology. She is such a nuisance.

Sadie and I cover all the main topics of conversation that real sisters do. Favourite *Friends* episode? My *The One with Ross's Tan* comes a close second to Sadie's *The One with Ross's Wedding*. I say that the *Lord of the Rings* trilogy is a horror movie. Sadie disagrees; she thinks that *Titanic* was 'way scarier' because everybody drowns. Sadie agrees that George Eliot should not have drowned Maggie Tulliver.

We go rogue and spend an hour internet shopping. The shops have reopened, but we like to be different, although Sadie calls this 'being difficult'. When it comes to making the most of your lumps and bumps, Sadie knows her stuff. She introduces me to body confidence dresses and their uses. Soon I have ordered six outfits, one for every day of the week (Sunday, I shall be naked).

'I know you dream of good hair days, but we beautiful ones can't have everything,' Sadie touches my locks (can she see my dreams now too?).

'Ha! Beautiful?' I laugh (I am *such* a people-pleasing, self-deprecating fool).

'Don't be greedy, Pippa. It wouldn't be fair on the rest of us if you had good hair days every day,' Sadie smiles. She is everything anyone could ever want in a sister.

Sadie does my makeup, but only after a severe face exfoliation opens and closes my pores.

'I'll be all dressed up, with nowhere to go,' I try not to look at myself in the mirror as Sadie contrives my face with colours too dark for my complexion.

'That's why I don't want you to waste any makeup on me.' Sadie knows what she's doing.

'Why not?' I ask.

'Because I have nowhere to go, Pippa.'

I have nothing to do this evening either, but I'm happy to keep quiet as Sadie improvises. The flat is filled with sounds that speak to me from years ago when I used to go out. I can be as strong as Amy, and my energy matches her challenging spirit. This comes from within; insipid does not influence power.

I try to focus on Sadie's face in the mirror as I remember the night it happened. I already smell of jasmine.

Last time was not the same as this time (Mummy's favourite subject). It was a dark winter's night, and The Peacock had said goodnight to its punters at least ten minutes earlier. I made my way downstairs to the bar as I needed to borrow something. I wore similar pyjamas to the ones I am wearing now. They may have been the same pair; I don't 'do sexy' very often. The night outside was cold and still. Then, there was a loud banging at the window, and I froze with the guilt of my crime.

I had not been caught stealing again; the intrusion turned out to be someone I knew. And as I opened the door to Tristan, I laughed. I laughed because he had given me a shock, I laughed because he had pleased me, and I laughed because I look good when I laugh. He had changed his mind; Tristan wanted me. All of my begging, bemoaning, and attention-seeking had finally worked. They say not to throw yourself at a man (especially not your best friend's husband), but I proved everyone wrong because Tristan surrendered. He wanted me when he propositioned me, and he wanted me the secret times that no one suspected. It wasn't my fault; none of this was my fault. Tristan was unable to resist what was naturally mine, and I was unable to stop it.

Drowning in a sea of guilt, Tristan left again to return to Cassandra's bed. The children must have been fairly young at the time (I bet they couldn't read). I never knew why India was walking along the road outside The Peacock that night. Sadie hinted she may have been coming to warn me against my unwise love match. It was my fault. The road was lit only by the car park lanterns seated at the bottom of old oak trees, and India met her death bouncing off the bonnet of Tristan's car.

All those lives were ruined in an instant. Not me; I chose to forget, and I've done such an excellent job of forgetting that I have managed to rewrite history. Turning responsibility off, I stayed at home until I was frumpy, fair, and nearly forty. Tristan would not have been out driving that night if it wasn't for me, and India would have been safe in her bed at home. Tristan would not have gone to prison for death by dangerous driving, and Cassandra would not have to pretend that her husband is 'working away'. Still, I should have known not to let her back in. The last few days have proved that Cassandra only befriended me because she wanted to teach me a lesson by taking Ben away.

I look at my mask in the mirror, and I know this is who I am; this is how I want to look.

Chapter Thirteen

S adie definitely put something in my coffee. I've been asleep all afternoon; she must have left during that time. Even if I say so myself, I still look fantastic (everyone does when they love themselves).

I'm all made up with nowhere to go, and I'm ready for bed in the pyjamas I have *saved for best.* Life is getting better, spring is trying to stretch into summer already, and I am completely safe. My secret will stay secret; why would I name a kitten after India if I was responsible for her death? That would be macabre.

I rolled in Sadie's fox fur, and it suits me. The best way to be is to pretend. The best way to smell is to copycat, and the best way to look is this. I look my best because Sadie looks this way.

I hear rattling downstairs. It must be India Kitten mischievously finding passage around our home (my four-legged baby).

'Pippa, are you in?'

It is Ben.

I don't answer because I don't know how to. When Ben reaches the top of the stairs, he has a sad little plastic carrier bag trailing between his legs. I realise he is alone, and it is then I know how to be. I am all dressed up and ready for bed.

Ben stands at the entrance to my flat, speaking a lot of words without really saying anything. He made a mistake. He still wants me. He thinks I'm amazing (he does not mention my makeover). I only hear what I want to hear; Cassandra didn't want him. She wants this pub. She thinks she's related to me. Cassandra was my half-sister's distant cousin or something. Didn't I know?

'Why did you use the past tense?' (And no, Ben – I didn't know.)

'What?' Ben says.

'You said Cassandra 'was' Sadie's cousin.' (The niece India wished to warn?)

'*Is*, then... Who is Sadie?' Ben says. He is still at the top of the stairs. 'I meant Heather, Pippa.'

'What?' Mummy would tell me to say *pardon*, but I need to speak to Ben on his own level.

'Cassandra is Heather's distant cousin or something. I can't believe you didn't know that.'

'I don't believe that for one second.' (And I can't wait to tell Sadie about this.)

'Look,' Ben steps forward and tries to slip his arms around my waist. I move away, but I don't resist. I don't want to resist. 'It was just... everything.'

'Everything?' I say.

'You know, lockdown,' Ben gazes down at my face with the look of national empathy. Why are all the men in my life using lockdown as an excuse?

(Apart from Mummy's husband, he doesn't believe in Covid.)

'So, the pandemic made you cheat on me?' I cannot believe how confident I sound. (I can't wait to tell Sadie.) Ben hugs my waist tighter and then lets me go (and lets himself into my front room).

'That's the thing, Pippa. I didn't cheat on you. That's what I'm on about. Cassandra doesn't want me; she wants this pub.'

'Wants this pub? This is Mummy's pub! I've lived here for as long as I can remember.' I need to put Ben straight. I thought John owned The Peacock, and then he married Mummy. Heather's father, Oswald was around too. And there was something about the brewery... I don't know anything about who owned the actual building. And Maddox, he had something to do with it somewhere along the line, like he had something to do with my conception. 'I can't wait to tell Sadie.'

'Pippa, why do you keep changing the subject? What do you think of what I said?'

'What do I think to what?' Mummy would turn in her happi coat if she could hear me forgetting to say pardon.

'I love you, and I want to come home to look after you.'

'What?' I must admit, Ben is looking very fit today.

'I'm sorry I went off the way I did, Pippa. I needed a bit of space because I just felt so redundant here. And Cassandra was always asking me to do things for her.' Ben's eyes start streaming.

'I noticed.' My face tells Ben I'm resolute. (I'm not; I've never seen his emotional side before.)

'She suggested I stay over that one night.' Ben recounts his tale like a reflective fabulist resting on his morals. 'She realised that I had drunk her coffee by mistake, and it had whisky in it. That's why I couldn't drive home. You must know how Cassandra feels about drink driving.'

I don't know how Cassandra feels about anything recently. Why is it that everyone in my life is flaunting their drink habit like a badge of honour? Ben's eyes give away his tears, and the tickling affliction creeps up my throat. 'Sadie said you *already* had a role here with me, Ben. *That's marriage for you,* she said.'

'What?' Ben realises he blurted out his question sharply and strokes the palm of my right hand. 'We're not... Who's Sadie, Pippa?'

'I told you, she's my half-sister's half-sister.'

'Heather is your sister.'

'I know, but Sadie is Heather's half-sister. Mummy is Heather's mummy as well as mine, but Heather shares a father with Sadie.' I talk to Ben as though he is stupid; he let Sadie in that day. Men always forget.

'And that dad-person had a wife called India,' Ben speaks to me as though I need an explanation about my extended, non-bloodline relatives.

Shit. Does this mean Ben knows my secret?

'Cassandra was related to India... somehow, she told me. I wasn't really listening... hang on, was there an adoption in there somewhere?' Ben's eyes are still red-rimmed. He does a half cough; I presume part of his *I wasn't listening to Cassandra* act. 'Pippa! You know I'm allergic to cats.' Ben's eyes widen as India Kitten resurfaces.

The tickling sensation had disappeared from my throat before Ben arrived home. It confidently returns with each mention of Sadie, and I can no longer keep the coughs away.

'See, you're affected by the cat too,' Ben reaches for the tissues. Am I still guilty for his secretions?

'She's my cat; her name is India,' I cough again.

'It's ok, we can take antihistamines,' Ben strokes my forearm. 'I can take care of it, Pippa, don't worry.'

Chapter Fourteen

The last thing I remember about yesterday is Ben telling me he wants to take care of me. We lie on the bed naked (and it's not even Sunday). I imagine we look like that scene in *When Harry Met Sally* where Meg Ryan looks satisfied, and Billy Crystal looks scared. Except I'm the scared one, this modern-day role reversal may not be all it seems. I'm feared because although Ben has returned, I am not sure he will want to stay.

'Morning beautiful, can I get you a cup of tea?' Ben kisses my neck. 'I am going to treat you like a princess from now on,' Ben has my left nipple in his mouth. 'I can't wait to look after you.'

I stop Ben's lips from wandering anywhere else. 'I'd better get up and feed India Kitten,' I sit up in bed (the bed that smells of Ben).

No, I'll take care of it, Pippa.

'Her,' I correct him (men always forget).

'I know, I meant *it* as in feed the kitten and sort out her litter tray.'

Who is this imposter?

'Don't look at me like that,' Ben's smile unleashes his dimples. 'I mean it; I want to take care of you. Every part of you, Pippa, and if you love cats then so do I. I've already started; I never even thought to take antihistamines before. They're great. I slept like a log.'

'I heard,' I tease Ben. He dandles my cheek like an aunt would, and we are back to normal again. When I return to work after these two weeks, nothing will have changed. I am frumpy, fair, and almost forty. Still a simpering people pleaser, still Ben's lover, and I can still read minds. When I return to my sums, Karen's face will tell me that my sister phoned the office (for an argument). I don't like change; I like to keep still.

'Everything is going to change around here, Pippa,' Ben returns to the bedroom with two cups of tea. He didn't read my mind. 'I mean it. I've decided to start a new project so that I can be your man, the actual man of the house.'

'What about the pub?'

'It's still closed, Pippa.'

'No one has said anything to me about The Peacock,' I say. No one has said anything to me about my flat either. I've lived here for as long as I can remember.

'Would you prefer to move away from here and choose a place together?' Big words from Ben.

'What about my family? Who will house sit Mummy's pub?' My words sound flimsy and I'm not quite sure what Ben thinks.

'You still can Pippa, I know I should have thought of this during last year, but it's time for us to settle down,' Ben cradles me like a child. I could get used to being looked after. Know little, question nothing, and relax. I wonder what Ben's job plans are. I wonder if this means being rich enough to give up working for Mr Bland. I wonder what life would be like without Karen.

'Don't do anything until I've gone back to work,' I beg.

'I won't, but how will I fill my time until next Monday?' Ben grins.

I hide in the safety of Ben's gaze for the rest of the day. I am Bathsheba Everdene, Ben is Gabriel Oak rising above the hedge to shepherd me into his care. Tristan is Boldwood, incarcerated because of me. Cassandra is Fanny Robin, buried under a thicket of dying flowers. Ben didn't choose Cassandra; she wanted to oust me from my home. None of this is my fault. It's like Sadie said, *'You already know what's happening; it's happening whether you like it or not'.* I like it. I want to accept it. Can instincts be trusted if they're driven by paranoia?

My bedroom is our bedroom again, and that's fine; I can never smell my own scent on myself. Getting ready for our reunited date night is difficult (silly really, Ben stayed away for less than a week and didn't even stray). I hate all my clothes again and have nothing to wear. My hair has abandoned the good times, and I can only hope this elastic hair band doesn't snap.

Ben enters the room dressed in a towel wrapped around his waist like a Celt boasting his iron conquest. Although I see him approach me from behind, I flinch with exhilaration when he caresses my bare buttock cheek. I am still deciding which dress to wear.

'You look gorgeous in purple,' Ben kisses my neck. I was hoping to wear black tonight.

'A compromise; it's sunny outside.' I pick up a summer number and slip it over my head. I look quite the bohemian when I add the right necklace.

Ben kisses the top of my head in approval, and my hair falls around my face.

'Oh!'

'Sorry,' Ben says. 'It looks better down.'

It doesn't look better down; any fool can see that. I look like candy floss on a fat stick. I turn around to make my way to the kitchen drawer, where I know hair accessories languish until I torture them. Ben stands in my way. 'Ben, I just want to get...'

'You're not going anywhere,' Ben grips me around the waist, loses his towel, and slips the dress back over my head. I can move away from him, but I don't want to. Ben's dark eyes look down on me, taking care to take in every part of my face. I look up at him hopefully, hoping he doesn't see the mess in front of him, hoping he didn't hear me blame him for the snapped hair tie. I have no idea what he's thinking. I miss Sadie.

'The doorbell!' I wriggle out of Ben's embrace, which he swiftly remedies. As quickly as he lost his modesty, the towel covers him again.

'I'll get it,' Ben says, with his unleashed dimples. 'I'm looking after you, remember... And no peeking until I'm ready for you.' Ben's face tells me he has a great idea, and before he bounds downstairs, I hear him lock the bedroom door.

To some, being locked in a room alone would be their worst nightmare. I really don't mind it; solitude can be comforting to a woman in a happy place. Trapped in a room knowing my lover is a metre away is strangely intoxicating. Who could be at the door? I hope Mummy hasn't given up on the lock situation again (or worse, my sister). If Ben was to greet Heather wearing nothing but tomorrow's laundry, her face would berate me until Christmas.

My ear is glued to the door. I wish I had a wine glass to help me listen; sobriety does have its downfalls. I think Ben is back upstairs, and he is alone (thankfully). I can hear him rearranging things in the kitchen (I must remember not to judge). As I curse my heart for pounding so loudly in my ears, Ben unlocks the bedroom door, and it opens in slow motion. Ben is wearing nothing but an apron (sadly, one of Heather's cast offs) and a tea towel draped over his right forearm. Unfortunately, I also see myself reflected in my mirrored wardrobe doors.

'Ben!' My dress is over my head again. 'Who was at the door?'

'It was a delivery driver for you,' Ben hands me a bountiful parcel that can only contain my rogue internet haul. I knew I should have chosen same-day delivery; today is the raison d'être of body confidence dresses.

'I just need to get changed,' I hug the package to my chest. Ben shakes his head no and leads me by the hand into my front room. This is the moment I realise why Ben said no peeking.

'You look just right, Pippa. Make yourself comfortable and let me take care of you.' Ben is fearless, and I am unable to resist. I see a candlelit table for two, including my missing wine glass. Ben has fashioned a heart-warming gesture; India Kitten munches biscuits in the corner.

'We're not going out?' I ask.

'No, it's your favourite, Pippa, staying in.' Ben's hand directs my gaze to a pasta dish and the surrounding cushioned asylum. 'And afterwards, we can watch whatever film you want. I'll even make popcorn.'

The smell of burst kernels and persuasion; my favourite.

Chapter Fifteen

I f Ben means what he says about choosing a new home together, I think I will insist on a bedroom with fewer mirrors. I often daydream of a different life, far ahead in time, finances, and geography. I sometimes think I choke my own fate in favour of the familiar. Today, I am unconcerned that any of this is my fault. Ben is asleep at the side of me with his mouth wide open, sucking in all the oxygen and breathing out noise.

I don't ever remember going this long without reading before. Seventy-two hours is a long time to hold your breath underwater. It's fine though, I shall float.

India Kitten attempts to open the bedroom door with her pink padded paw. Ever the people pleaser, I surrender my lie-in for quality feline time (and allow my lover his sleep). This is the way I fuss my cat on a lazy weekend morning. I watch her quench her thirst, pooling water from the bowl in her tiny paw (India Kitten is yet too small to dunk her face). I watch her enjoy dry biscuits, inhaling brown shapes as though her mouth is a silver trowel. I expect her to jump on my lap and curl in satisfaction. But India Kitten does not. Instead, she delicately makes her way around the flat. I wonder what goes on inside this cat's mind. How does she decide on her next move? Padding across the laminate, India Kitten attempts to climb the walls. Agility allows her onto the landing window-sill that faces Mummy's house, and I am struggling to read her. No matter, I have fallen in love with India Kitten. I accept inevitable aloofness, yet I am sure the bond of imprinting is mutual.

'India Kitten, what are you doing?' I coo gently into the back of her head (my favourite small space is between an animal's ears). The cat ignores me, choosing to dart her eyes around the outside. 'You're too young for adventures just yet.' Two weeks is the standard time to keep a cat in-side; I may extend this to *forever* in India Kitten's case. The road outside The Peacock was quiet dur-ing the lockdown; I could have sunbathed on the tarmac. I almost did until Heather popped around with a joke about my freckles. This year, traffic has returned, and much more than the occasional de-livery driver uses our road as a thoroughfare.

Mummy interrupts my serenity by frantically waving from her opposite awning window. I wave back. She tries to shout over to me, ducking her head towards the bottom opening. I can't hear her. No doubt Mummy expects me to stand on her driveway and listen. Her fist knocks on the upper pane of glass, and her eyes widen. I pull at my py-jamas with forefingers and thumbs; can't Mummy see I am in a state of undress? She doesn't care, beckoning me over as though I'm a serving wench. (Where is Heather when I need her?)

Fortunately, the weather and time of year allows for a big coat. Multitude of sins hidden, I slip on my boots and prepare to leave the pub. India Kitten has followed me. 'Oh, now you want to snuggle?' she looks straight through me, purring and waiting for the door to open. I've owned cats before, and I know how to be stealth-like. After a few trips up and down the stairs (while carefully maintaining the quiet for Ben), India Kitten is safely herded away, and I make my escape.

As I turn around, Mummy has disappeared from her window. Good, she must be on her way downstairs to let me in – much more civilised than a driveway conversation. It is only when I shut The Peacock's main door behind me that I realise I do not have my key. Mummy has not appeared at her doorway, but I hear my phone ringing inside The Peacock.

It must be Mummy; no one ever contacts me on my landline. I am stuck in the middle of the road. I wish this coat had a hood. If Mummy uses her landline to connect with mine, she won't be anywhere near her upstairs window. Yet, if I return to The Peacock, I can't open the door. This is my worst nightmare going round and round, keeping Ben's return a secret and obeying my mother.

There is no answer when I knock on Mummy's door. I can hear her voice; it is raised in good humour. Maybe she wasn't trying to connect with me... whoever she is speaking to is receiving the Jacquetta treatment. I imagine her smoothing her hair behind her ear as she laughs. I hadn't imagined seeing Ben at the flat's window, but there he is with India Kitten in one hand, and the phone up to his ear. I step backwards, and damn it, Mummy has returned to her upstairs window. She notices me, and her face gives me mock surprise. She bats me away and flashes a smile in Ben's direction. He waves and disappears. It is as though Mummy already knew of his return.

I miss Sadie.

Ben opens The Peacock's door, welcoming me into my own home as though nothing has changed. 'Your mum has been trying to get hold of you,' Ben speaks as though he had never left. Those two sets of seventy-two hours didn't happen. Six days of my holiday have disappeared into the chasm of *where does the time go?*

'I know, Ben. She was waving me over at her window but didn't open her front door.'

Ben teases me, rubbing a towel over my wet head. 'She can't open her door; she's lost her keys.'

'Lost her keys?' I repeat.

'Yes, she blames her cat, and John blames your mother.' When we are safely inside, Ben lets India Kitten down onto the floor. He wipes his hands on his (recently acquired) jeans, but I don't mind; he has dimples.

'How can Patrice be responsible for lost keys? And was Mummy surprised when you answered the phone?' This is all very strange.

'No, she saw me at the window, didn't she?' Ben smiles at me. Nothing has changed. He knows all about Mummy and her keys and her cat, and Mummy appears to know all about Ben. This is the way we stand in silence on a cold and drizzly morning. 'I expect that's her ringing your mobile,' Ben nods towards the bedroom. Great, along with Mummy's sudden indifference towards Ben, I am wet with rain and cold in my pyjamas.

'Hello,' I sigh.

'Hello to you too, Epiphany, we're having a nightmare over here. An absolute nightmare!' Mummy is too harassed to be worried about Ben. 'I've just told your young man about the cat hiding the keys. We have been locked in here for twenty-four hours, Epiphany. An outrage!' Mummy did not take heed of last year's lockdown, so being locked in with her husband is understandably terrible. 'And your phone has been on the blink...'

'No, it hasn't,' I look at my phone – everything seems in order, and Ben answered the landline when she called a few minutes ago.

'This is just like last time.' Mummy moans.

'No, it isn't.' I can tell Mummy is clutching her necklace.

'It is; I couldn't unlock the door on the night... Is Ben in the room with you?' Mummy whispers.

'No,' I look in the mirror to make sure I'm

alone. Ben is in the kitchen, dutifully taking care of me. 'Had you spoken to Ben, Mummy?'

'Yes, he just answered the phone. This is a nightmare, Epiphany; I hope there is no funny business going on again.'

'He wants me back, Mummy, and I found him too difficult to resist.' I meant had Mummy spoken to Ben before today.

'What? What are you talking about? I'm referring to the night poor India died; I couldn't unlock my door then either... all I could do was watch the blue lights through the window, and you, Epiphany made things worse. Wailing on the road telling anyone who would listen that it wasn't your fault.' Mummy forgets her prior disapproval of 'poor' India. She has also forgotten to whisper. Fortunately, Ben has the kettle on and is whistling while he watches it boil. I close the bedroom door just in case.

'Mummy,' I whisper harshly, but she cuts me off.

'Epiphany, no amount of prayers to the patron saint of keys can release me this time.'

'You're not religious, Mummy. Are you?' Is she?

'What else could I do, Epiphany?' I can hear her pacing up and down. 'That reminds me, have you...?'

'Have I what?' My cup of tea will be going cold if Mummy keeps me in this ridiculous conversation for much longer.

'I noticed one of those blue bottles outside

The Peacock. It must have smashed in the frost. It was icy this year, wasn't it?'

'What blue bottle?' I have no idea what Mummy means.

'You must remember. I only noticed it because of all the gazing out at stolen freedom,' Mummy is so dramatic. 'It was after *last time,*' Mummy is getting on my last nerve. 'You found a smashed bottle in the pub car park. Heather swears that bottles are hung from trees on the African continent to ward off evil spirits.'

'It probably came from downstairs.' I don't know where Mummy is going with this, and I don't think she does either.

'Well, it's alright for those in Africa. Their bottles are unlikely to crack during a cold and frosty winter,' Mummy beats around the bush. 'It must be where all the bad luck is coming from.'

'What bad luck?' I see no bad luck. Ben has not forsaken me after all, and Cassandra has a misunderstanding about The Peacock. I am on holiday.

'Not being able to unlock my door, of course. Are you listening, Epiphany?' Mummy is telling me off now. Ben gently nudges the door open, but only to let India Kitten in. He passes me a cup of tea and performs a cheeky eye roll.

'Yes, I'm listening.'

'Fetch the spare key over then!'

'I don't have your spare key. You've telephoned the wrong daughter.' How good it feels to point out Mummy's failings in favouring Heather.

'Heather lives in Pendle, Epiphany,' Mummy does not acknowledge my meaning. 'There is a spare key to my house behind the bar downstairs. Oh, by the way, before this happened, John noticed a sign about a missing kitten. It looks just like the one I've seen pawing your windows during the past few days. I didn't want to say anything at first because of the lease problem. Anyway, there you are. Pop the spare key through the letterbox, won't you?'

Chapter Sixteen

Back I go over the road. My staycation will be wasted going round and round. Hopefully, Mummy will shed some light on the (various) conversation starters she dropped at my door just now. I have often thought that Mummy is into magical thinking, but praying to the patron saint of keys? Is that a Catholic thing? I don't believe Mummy is Catholic; I went to a public comprehensive school.

I don't believe India Kitten is the same cat on the notice John found. Mummy and John claim to have been locked away; the missing kitten has probably been found by now. This must be Mummy plotting to either make me sans feline, or maybe Patrice is with kitten after all, and she needs a foster parent. I noticed Mummy mentioned the 'lease' again. In any case, Sadie would not gift me a purloined pussy cat; she is my half-sister's half-sister.

The most unbelievable thing is that Mummy appears to have changed her tune regarding Ben's suitability. This is even less likely than Mummy's smashed bottle theory. I need to get to the bottom of this.

Mummy's front doors are locked as always; nothing has changed there. A spidery set of fingers poke through the redundant letterbox. The notice about the missing cat is paper planed across the porch floor. Brilliant; I can't reach it but can make out the corner of a photograph with the same colour as India Kitten's ear. This means nothing; cats are black, white, or ginger... or tortoiseshell. It probably isn't her.

An unravelled wire coat hanger pokes through the letterbox with no sense of urgency (it's still raining). I hear a muffled *'throw the keys onto the floor'* echoing around the porch. I hear Mummy's shrill protestations and John's deep capability. Eventually, the wire is successful in retrieving the keys. I wait for Mummy to unlock her door, but nothing happens. I stay on the wrong side of Mummy's porch for longer than I care to. Rain bursts heavily on my head and whips me in the face. I hear more muffled voices from inside, and I cannot distinguish what is being said at either end of the decibel scale. After a while, I decide to return to The Peacock. I doubt I would get any answers had I spoken to Mummy face to face. Without Heather, Jacquetta would skirt around the issue of my love life, my 'lease', and would agree with Heather about African superstition. I never win. Here we go round the stumbling block on an awkwardly stilted morning.

I hear sneezing upstairs when I return home. This time, Ben is not at the front door ruffling my wet hair. The tickling sensation in my throat prevents me from shouting up to him, but all is well. Ben is herding India Kitten to safety, as I had earlier. Here he comes down the stairs flashing his dimples. This is the way I like my boyfriend; 'let me take care of that,' he removes my coat on this cold and rainy morning.

After a lavish breakfast (made by Ben), I wonder what we will do for the rest of the day. Ben appears unconcerned by any forward planning. Despite his speech about taking care of me, he doesn't seem to have done anything about it yet. I regret halting his enthusiasm by asking him to wait until I return to work. I suppose I shouldn't complain; he is doing the washing up and, as far as I know, hasn't heard a peep from Cassandra.

Speaking of... Where is Sadie? I try to count the days since I last saw her. It was the day of my makeover, and (not only because of the rain) I worry I can't maintain my new look. I enjoyed the time I spent with Sadie so much that I didn't think to ask her for her phone number. I must look for her on social media later.

'I'll get it,' Ben shouts from the other end of the flat. I hear him running downstairs, shutting the interior door behind him. I swear I didn't hear the doorbell, and a book is in my hands. I haven't been reading it. Just skim reading – I hate it when that happens. Ben swings around the banister rail at the top of the stairs. 'Oh, by the way, Pippa, I need to speak to you about borrowing some money for my new venture.'

Not an imposter, then.

I hear muffled voices again, and this time it is Heather's tone of disapproval. It will be unclear how she feels about Ben until she reaches the top step (Heather always sounds objectionable).

'I see you've employed a butler, Pippa. Always was free and easy with other people's belongings,' Heather greets me without a greeting, and I don't know if she meant Ben or me. This is my flat, and up until recently, I have never had cause to consider who it actually belongs to.

'I'll be Pippa's butler if she'll have me,' Ben slips onto the couch next to me and removes the book from my lap. Heather sticks her finger in her mouth and mimics retching. She is so uncouth.

'Would you like a drink, Heather?' I offer.

'I'll get it,' Ben dashes off to the kitchen. My kettle has never seen so much action since his return.

'I've come about this kitten, Pippa,' Heather looks around the room as though I have hidden India.

'You could have come earlier, have you been to Mummy's?' Of course, she has.

'I couldn't come earlier. I have a family to look after remember,' Heather sometimes conveniently forgets this fact herself when tempted by Mummy's charms. I reveal India Kitten's whereabouts by reaching down to her basket. Rubbing the knuckle of my forefinger across my favourite space, she begins to purr.

'Tea or coffee, Heather?' Ben shouts.

'Tea, please, and make it weak, won't you?' Heather likes it feeble and tasteless. 'Jacquetta gave me this flyer about a lost kitten. She tells me she's been watching your window while she and John have been locked away, and your secret kitten looks like this one.'

'She only lost her keys for one day,' I say.

'Look,' Heather ignores me. 'Look at the picture; it definitely looks like this kitten. Pippa, a child has lost its pet. How can you be so cruel?'

Heather and Mummy have been colluding again. I must be assertive and decide against revealing that India Kitten was a gift from Sadie.

'Where did you get it?'

Shit, has Heather read my mind?

'She's a *her*! Pippa doesn't like it if you call the cat 'it',' Ben returns like a dutiful obedient, saving me from Heather's questioning with mugs of tea. Heather starts attacking me with the leaflet again.

'Look at this poster, Pippa. You didn't even look properly. You're always the same, burying your head in the sand and pretending you're without fault.' Heather parents me, and I take the leaflet from her. The face of a cat that admittedly looks remarkably like India Kitten gazes back at me.

'This kitten is called Patch. That's a boy's name, Heather.' Problem solved, now Heather can go away and leave Ben and me to our day.

'Pippa, we should at least check with the owners of this kitten,' Heather points at India rather than the photograph of Patch. 'They only live around the corner on the estate. And Patch is not a boy's name; Pippa, it's unisex.'

'Every Patch I've known has been a male,' Ben defends me.

'Thank you, but this is between me and Pippa.'

Not Pippa and I, but me and Pippa. My sister looks around the room again, measuring up my windows for roller blinds.

'What are you wearing, anyway?' Heather is such a cow, and Ben agrees because he raises his eyebrows and darts out of the room.

'A new dress,' I defend.

'You look like... You look just like...' Sadie's name is on the tip of Heather's tongue. 'What did you name *this* kitten then?'

'India.'

'That is macabre,' said Heather.

Chapter Seventeen

'I expect you feel quite foolish, Pippa,' Heather has a way with words.

The thing is, I have felt foolish for the majority of my life. I think Heather is referring to something specific, though, and we have only the slope in the middle of the new estate to walk to solve the riddle. Around the corner from The Peacock sits a sprawling jungle of forty-year-old concrete. These suburban mouse traps are only a fraction of the age of Mummy's house and the pub. That's why we call it the new estate, and this is where my cat rival lives. 'Why am I foolish?' I venture.

Heather stops dead in the road and turns to me. I stop walking, and India Kitten meows in her carrier. 'Because Cassandra didn't want Ben, you silly girl,' Heather shakes her nose in my face as though to nuzzle me.

I know Cassandra didn't want Ben; she wants the pub. But neither Heather nor I say this. Instead, Heather says something which makes me feel truly guileless.

'She used Ben for the odd jobs she had knocking around her house,' Heather is pleased with herself. I resist treating her to the *contretemps with Cassandra* story (Heather is not a patch on Sadie's sympathy). I remain silent; my sister is used to this because things often go unsaid between us. 'There is a reason she needed her house tarting up... You're very quiet, Pippa. Don't you want to know what I've found out?'

I sigh a medium weight sigh at Heather. My annual leave is wasted on draining conversations.

'Tristan is back, Pippa. Tristan is home with Cassandra and the children. You silly, silly girl.' Heather laughs, turns, and continues dragging me towards my usurper's house. I'm not a girl; I'm frumpy, fair, and my heart is in my mouth. I wonder what will happen if Tristan pays me a visit now that he's home. I had no idea about the length of his stretch; I have no idea about the penal system. I know I'm guilty, but I'm not the one who got caught. He's not a free man, though. No doubt he confessed to Cassandra that he was here after closing time at The Peacock. I have driven myself round the twist blaming myself and then blaming Tristan for the accident. Ultimately, I was the one who made his blood boil and impassioned him to the point of riskiness. Tristan kept making the same mistakes but expected different answers.

Heather snaps her fingers before my eyes 'Epiphany,' she shouts. We're here; this is the house. India Kitten meows, probably in protest. There is not a chance she isn't my cat; everyone knows that cats find their owners, and India Kitten found me.

As we walk up the path, I am reminded that Heather is all things to all people. She inspects the Sparks family's choice of shrubs and resists her urge to deadhead a rose with her bare fingers. She smoothes her hair by sliding her rose-coloured spectacles to the top of her head as she knocks on the door. 'Mrs Sparks?' I see Heather's mouth move, but I hear Jacquetta's voice. Heather is all things to all people. Always. Today, she has decided to mimic Mummy. Two can play that game.

'Yes,' Mrs Sparks answers. Her eyes dart from Heather to me, to the cat carrier and back again. Her eyebrows don't move as I expect them to; still, Heather is yet to perform.

'Hello there, my name is Heather. This is my sister,' Heather introduces herself and acknowledges me with a slight flicker. I have started to shake but give my best straight shoulders and a pleasant closed-mouth smile. 'We've come about the flyer,' Heather produces the 'missing kitten' flyer with a flick of her wrist. 'I hope this isn't an imposition?'

'No! No, it isn't,' Mrs Sparks looks behind her and pulls her door closed. She reaches towards India Kitten's carrier. I must have moved it because suddenly I am between Mrs Sparks and India Kitten. I am waiting for Heather to explain that we would like to check the contents of the cage before (unnecessarily) handing her over. I am unclear if Heather disapproves of my attempts to hide India Kitten or wants me to speak.

'I have been looking after this kitten,' I gesture behind me. 'For quite a while, and if it's no...' I sound drunk, and I can't think of a Jacquetta way of asking. 'Would you mind, awfully, if I check with you... if you think this cat is your missing kitten?' I enunciate my words slowly and as Mummy-like as possible. This is the way I pretend to be on this people-pleasing morning.

'My sister has been looking after her; we were worried she had escaped from her 'proper' owners.' Heather colludes and implies my 'improperness'. She is giving a fine Jacquetta performance.

'I did wonder if she had an owner,' I slur.

'Well,' Mrs Sparks moves gently towards me, as though I am a frightened cub with sharp claws. 'Our daughter wanted a kitten for a long time, and we eventually gave in, you know what kids are like. That's how we ended up with Mrs Patch. But my daughter let her out too early; she said she wanted to take her for a walk in the garden.' This woman does not deserve a cat. 'Could I have a look?' Mrs Sparks puts her head on one side.

'Perhaps it would be a good idea if your daughter carried out the identification if it's not too much trouble?' Damn it, I should have used the word *imposition*. Why am I so shaky? Heather turns to me with widened eyes and then turns back to Mrs Sparks.

'Oh, I don't think that will be necessary. I'm sure Mrs Sparks can recognise her own cat,' Heather dismissively laughs, and Mrs Sparks joins her. The kitten carrier is snatched from me, and

Mrs Sparks unfastens the catches. On reflection, I agree it is unwise to get the child's hopes up (although she only has herself to blame for this, cats do not go for walks with humans).

'My daughter is seven years old,' Mrs Sparks adds, I presume to help us understand why she would be so careless with her long-coveted pet. I have no sympathy; I was reading at eleven months. 'Do you want to come out?' Mrs Sparks applies high pitched persuasion, and India Kitten leads with her nose. She paws the woman like a long-lost friend. 'There,' India Kitten immediately settles in the woman's shoulder. 'Thank you for bringing her back,' Mrs Sparks thanks Heather. 'And for looking after her,' she adds in child-like tones for my benefit.

'Is she definitely your cat?' I protest. I read Heather's mind, and she kicks me under the imaginary table.

'Of course, she is!' Heather turns me around in the driveway. 'I hope we haven't caused your daughter too much distress. I think my sister thought she was doing the right thing.' Heather narrows her eyes and nods as she says the last two words. I *was* doing the right thing, Sadie gifted me a kitten, and I fell in love with her. This is the way I must believe the cat belongs to the Sparks family.

I put Jacquetta on again and try one last appeal. 'Would your daughter mind if I visit India Kitten occasionally... if it's not too much of an alliteration?' Shit. I've got the wrong word.

Mrs Sparks tries desperately to raise her eyebrows, and I read *not a chance* in the rest of her face. 'Sorry, I need to go back in; I can hear my daughter calling for me.' Mrs Sparks either has excellent hearing, or she is lying. I hear no child shouting *Mummy*, but I do hear the sound of a car rolling onto the driveway. I've never seen a wife so pleased to see her husband.

'Hello,' Mr Sparks shuts his driver's door, making the delicious clunking sound found only in expensive cars.

'Hello, darling, good news, the kitten is back!' Mrs Sparks retreats from her escape. I notice that India Kitten is fidgeting and plucking her shoulder.

'Oh, that's brilliant. See, I told you missing cat posters work,' Mr Sparks grins.

Missing cat posters? This couple are a pair of fraudsters... I bet they have collected many cats and kittens and have a sick fur factory inside their house. I try to say something, but I am unable. Heather has me transfixed, and I don't wish to risk a lengthy and tedious lecture on herbs that can help balance moods.

'Hang on, I recognise you two, don't I?' Does he? I've never seen this kitty-napper in my life before. He distracted me, and Mrs Sparks has disappeared inside with India Kitten (again without the proffered sound of offspring). 'You guys run the pub down the road, don't you?'

'Oh, yes, yes, our mother... So sorry, I didn't recognise you at first, Mr Sparks,' Heather says. I'm unsure if she reached out her hand to invite Mr Sparks to kiss it because I am trying to look over her shoulder at the door.

'When is it reopening then?' Mr Sparks says. He has forgotten why we are here and has failed to thank us for adding to his pelt collection.

Heather replies with something that sounds like *it isn't* before marching me away from the house of boxes (and I didn't get the chance to say goodbye to India Kitten).

I must remember to search for Sadie on social media when I arrive home.

Chapter Eighteen

'Don't forget, Pippa, tomorrow is the women's retreat. Remember, I promised to go with you.' Heather speaks as though she is doing me a favour. She has lost her Jacquetta cover, and I want to lose mine. I need to put Sadie on and tell Heather that there is not a chance of me attending menopause yoga. She has just made me give up the love of my life. India Kitten is gone, and I am sans feline.

I make a sound between agreement and distress. The empty kitty carrier bangs against my legs as I walk, berating me for the foolish ninny that I am.

'Don't cry, Pippa. Have you been crying a lot recently? I was the same when I was perimenopausal.'

'No.' I try to sound carefree, but I know my vibe is crumbling.

'It wasn't that long ago, Pippa that you were crying a *lot*. Women can be perimenopausal for ten years before the actual menopause, did you know that?' Heather makes things up, blames it on hormones, and makes me feel prepubescent all in one sentence.

'No,' a one-word answer is the way forward with Heather.

'The women's retreat will help you. The breathing exercises are to die for, and the women who run it are experts in yoga and reiki.'

Honestly, a woman as accomplished as Heather does talk as though she is thick sometimes. 'Help me with what? They can't bring India back, can they?' I say.

'You don't need her now; Ben is back. He never left, not really, so there is no need for this emotional breakdown, tears in the cat litter, and so on. It is hormones, Pippa making you feel like this. You just need a good old fashioned spiritual unblocking... So, shall I meet you there, or do I have to drive all the way here to collect you?' Heather gives me two questions, and where I was planning on saying 'no', I now have to make a choice.

'I'll drive myself there,' I say in a small voice.

'Good girl,' Heather gives me a restrained hug, jarred at the elbows. 'Have you been drinking?'

'No, and I thought you didn't like Ben.'

'I don't. Stop trying to change the subject, Pippa. Are you sure you haven't been drinking?' Heather school-mistresses me.

'No, I don't drink,' I say. Heather gives me a look, and I can't tell what she's thinking. I daren't argue with her, not even inside my head.

'OK,' Heather pats my upper arms. 'Now that returning the kitten is all sorted, I can go home to my brood.' Heather releases me from her grip and turns in the direction of Mummy's house. 'Oh, don't forget, Pippa. Part of the retreat is ecstatic dance, so dress accordingly.'

'I don't want to do enforced dancing,' I plead.

'Don't be an imbecile, Pippa. No one is forcing you to do anything,' Heather makes her escape; no doubt she will update Mummy on their get rid of India plan. The cat carrier and I turn to make our way into The Peacock. Shit, I've just realised I didn't ask Heather what she meant by *it isn't* (re-opening). I presume I will continue to live in my flat. Eventually, the bar snacks will run out, but that's fine; I shall send Ben out for some. Unless he dumps me again, in that case, I shall be making my own 'missing kitten' posters; it worked for Mr and Mrs Sparks.

Heather and Mummy own cats. Mummy has Patrice, and Heather has so many mousers in her outdoor structures that I forget their names and get them mixed up with my nieces and nephews. They probably see cat ownership as familiar company rather than a knee jerk adoption. I feel judged and heartbroken; I loved India Kitten. She was a gift from Sadie... I miss Sadie. I wonder what Heather meant by remembering me crying 'a lot'.

I reach the top of the stairs, and the need to be held overwhelms me. I'm a bit out of breath and start coughing. Ben has propped open the front door to the flat with a book. One of my books.

'Hello,' Ben shouts from inside the flat. 'How did it go? Did they seem like nice people?' I hear the sound of a vacuum cleaner banging against skirting boards. I open my mouth to ask Ben *what brought this on*, but the tickling sensation has garrotted me. I make a sound between confirmation and disapproval, grab the book from the door and escape to the bathroom. As the flat's door slams shut, another is left open. I try to quell my spurting rasps; it must be the dust. While I am here, I may as well use the facilities. Ben must be joking! The book he used to wedge open the door is Aunt India's *Book of Fantastic Facts*.

This is the way I hack my heart out, sitting in the bathroom.

'Are you OK, Pippa?' Ben approaches the bathroom, and I am worried about black mascara streaming down my face. I cover my head with a towel, which billows out with my barks. 'Shut the door, Pippa!' I feel a draft as Ben traps me in (Sadie didn't mind me leaving the bathroom door open).

'Always,' I finally get my words out. 'I'm always OK...Why are you propping the door open with my book?' I really should be relaying to Ben how bereft I'm feeling about the loss of India Kitten. Then he can make a start on consoling me (I was her foster mother for at least seventy-two hours).

'I thought I'd make a start on getting the cat smell out of here,' Ben says. His voice disappears around the flat. India Kitten made no smell at all; I don't know what Ben is talking about. 'I hope we sleep tonight without those antihistamines.' Ben is so matter of fact about my loss that I start to feel myself get annoyed. It is a good job that I am hidden away because my face is giving away all kinds of cursing glares. I must remember I want Ben to stay.

'I hope so too,' I am great at smoothing things over. 'I'm going to that women's retreat thing with Heather tomorrow; I don't want to be tired,' I miss Sadie, I miss India. I am tired after a day of being all things to all people.

'That's nice. What time will you be home?' Ben takes an interest in me. I wonder if he knows about Tristan.

'I'm not sure, probably late afternoon,' I guess. I resist asking why Ben wants to know my expected time of return.

'I thought I could cook again... I thought about taking you out for a nice meal, but there's something I need to talk to you about, so it's better if we're here.'

Not this shit again.

'Don't look so worried, Pippa,' Ben grabs my hand and kisses it. 'I've got an idea, but I'll need to borrow some money to put my plan into action.'

'Why? What is it?' I hope I'm not wrong about Ben; I suppose he won't have time for Cassandra if he's busy with a project. Even with Tristan home, I don't trust her.

'Let me tell you tomorrow, I will meet with my guy while you're out with Heather. Then we can talk about it. It's for our future, Pippa. I need to take care of you. We will have to spend money to make money, though.'

We? I thought Ben wanted to borrow money rather than a joint spending spree? 'I'm tired,' I say, attempting to remain amicable. 'Do you mind if we have an early night tonight?'

'No,' Ben unleashed his dimples with his smile and ruffles my hair. I do wish he would stop doing that.

Maybe I went to bed too early. Perhaps the lack of antihistamines has stopped me from sleeping through. I would not have formed a habit in seventy-two hours, would I? It is half-past one in the morning, and there is not an ounce of sleep in me. I wish I could drive to Heather's retreat right now and get it over with because I am wide awake. This reminds me of the summer I found out I'm allergic to alcohol. It was worse, but not as bad. Night after night, I would gaze at my ceiling with my eyes closed. Awake, because what knocked me out initially woke me with dehydration four or five hours later. Maybe this is what Mummy and Heather meant by *last time*. Except... I am a private person and don't remember sharing my habits with those two.

Maybe I should get out of bed and have a glass of water. Or a glass of milk... or a bottle of wine to knock me out... waking again at dawn with a thirst is perfect for a day of hippy shit. Hair of the dog would be welcome under the circumstances; it might help me get through the enforced dancing.

No, I can't persuade myself that easily. Glass of water it is...

This didn't work and is followed by a trip to the bathroom an hour later. I dare to switch the light on and notice *The Book of Fantastic Facts* on the side. I never did get to find out what Sadie's superpower is, and telepathy has eluded me of late. I wonder what Sadie is doing right now. I wonder what Tristan is doing. I wonder if he and Cassandra were pleased to see each other. My ears were burning before I went to bed. I hope they didn't spend their first night together plotting revenge. I know I will always fear bumping into either one of them. Always. That's why I should stay here. Although, didn't Ben say that Cassandra wants this pub? What does that mean? I'm going round in circles; I need to see Sadie and ask if it's true. Is Cassandra her half-sister's half-cousin or something? Perhaps I should read a book...maybe I should read all the books.

I turn to the last page read from my currently reading pile and fail to recall the words. Do I remember everything from all the books I have read? A look through something more memorable should send me off. I have never read *Strange Case of Dr Jekyll and Mr Hyde*, but I cannot resist another dip into Aunt India's book.

The trivia encyclopaedia uncovered an urban myth about a dentist who hid his alcohol dependency by drinking neat vodka from mouthwash cups all day long. And a famous handbag designer made their first tote at age eleven (I bet she couldn't read at eleven months, though).

I wake up gritting my teeth after a vivid dream, as clear in my mind as my skin is since I stopped drinking. India was Jacquetta, and Sadie was Heather. That's how I knew it was a dream. I wore a blindfold, and when Sadie lifted this veil, I realised where I was. My flat and The Peacock had been replaced by a carousel. A moat without a drawbridge stood in between here and Mummy's house. Cassandra trod water, struggling to float but refusing to drown. Weirdly, Tristan drove the merry-go-round. He smelt like a brewery, but it was the day after smell, tart and sour, and seeping from his pores. I was trapped going round and round in circles. I think that's why I gritted my teeth.

I don't remember seeing Ben in the dream, but he is right here next to me now, his sleep undisturbed by the lack of antihistamines.

Chapter Nineteen

Waking with memories always spooks me. Always. Someone once told me that prophetic dreams are uncommon (it may have been Karen from work). Believing most things that people tell me, I ignore nightmares and hallucinations, but dreams always come back to haunt me.

I must get my hair done.

I pad from my bed towards the kitchen to brew some coffee. I need to start today with some clarity; I make it strong enough to unblock sleepy intrusions. I gaze out of the window and blow on my hot drink; the glass steams my window and hides Mummy's house. Taking in the early morning, I hope against all hope that I catch a glimpse of India Kitten. There is a possibility that the Sparks weren't lying about her being a family cat.

As the fog disappears, I see the silhouette of a cat pawing the inside of Mummy's upstairs window. The cat manages to defeat the blinds and stands on her back paws to scare her prey. It is Patrice, and she is interested in the window because there is a magpie on the other side of it. Damn it, I will have to remain here and wait for another one to come along.

The magpie appears to ignore Patrice but is aggressively curious about something on the ledge outside the window. It flutters its black and white wings, bobbing its head in defiance of Patrice, who is now tangled in a blind toggle. A pair of hands (I think I recognise as John's) reach in behind the blind and scoop Patrice away. The magpie stays and is joined by a mate who is also drawn to the ledge. I am grateful for the *two for joy* and can now start getting ready for a day of hippy shit with Heather. Yet, I don't move because something lands around Mummy's window that I have hoped for since the night of the accident.

Seven mischievous magpies titter around Mummy's window bringing good tidings of a secret never to be told. I am free. No one need ever know I was the reason Tristan was driving that night. I never have to tell anyone my part in India's death because seven is a secret never to be told.

'Oh!' I squeal as Ben surprises me from behind and grabs me around my waist. I've noticed I am jumpy these days. Perhaps Heather is right; maybe I do need menopause yoga.

'Where's my cup of tea?' Ben says.

'It's coffee; you don't like coffee.'

'I'm only joking, don't worry. I'll take care of it.' Ben overfills the kettle and reaches for the teabags. I carry on watching Mummy's house. Nothing has changed, but everything is better. Another set of workmen arrive in their van. I regret telling Heather I would drive today; workmen always tell me how to reverse out of The Peacock's driveway. Always. They point their fingers round and round as though the jalopy's steering wheel is alien to me.

Today's workmen wear dirty overalls that look like spent forensic suits. With hands in the small of their backs, they look up towards the parliament of magpies and perform a collective whistle of dread. Soon, Mummy is out on the drive wearing her happi coat, nodding in agreement about the circulating building emergency. I read that a resolution is offered, and then grey dust sheets and ladders are hauled out of their van. Mummy is always having something done to her house. Always. She has a conservatory on her lean-to and a corridor that leads nowhere upstairs, leaving her visitors to search in spirals for the bathroom door.

'Are you looking out for magpies again?' Ben is behind me, and now we are both spying on Jacquetta. My entire holiday is filled with people commentating on what I'm doing *again*.

'I was; there were seven on Mummy's windowsill before. Then I noticed the workmen arrive, and now there's only one.'

'Do seven magpies mean a secret or something?' Ben pretends not to know the rhyme that everyone knows.

'A secret never to be told,' I remind him.

'Sounds sexy,' Ben says (I don't know where he

gets sexy from). 'What about two for joy?'

'Yes, Mr Magpie and his wife were on Mummy's window before.'

'Has anything joyful ever happened after you've seen two magpies?' Ben folds his arms.

'No... I don't think so; I'm not that much of a lucky person.' I genuinely always forget to look out for the finer things after spotting two magpies.

'Well, you don't need to believe that one magpie will bring you sorrow then, not if two has never brought you joy.' Ben has a point.

'I do feel joy, though; the joy of seeing two magpies.'

'I'm glad because you were really sad yesterday about the cat,' Ben smiles at me. Then he points at Heather's car arriving on Mummy's driveway. 'I thought you said you were driving yourself to that thing today?'

I make a sound between one for sorrow and two for joy. The joy that I won't have to reverse the jalopy in front of Mummy's workmen and the sorrow that Heather has come to pick me up. None of this is my fault.

'I thought I was driving?' I shout from my window. Heather gives me a look of the penny dropping mixed with annoyance at her own mistake. Whenever Heather has occasion to blame me for her martyrdom, she must employ Mummy as a witness. I watch her ringing Jacquetta's doorbell. Mummy has only just returned inside after instructing today's minions. Her face is animated when Heather reports on my inconvenience. St Heather is canonised once again by Jacquetta, and I disappear inside my flat.

I have paid handsomely for a day of female bonding, enough to keep the hippies in braziers for the foreseeable. Ben kisses me goodbye at The Peacock, and I read approval in his eyes. I may have been spared back seat reversing this morning, but as I pass the workmen, I read humour and surprise in their minds.

'Good grief, Pippa! What are you wearing?' Heather shouts at me. I look down at myself, and the workmen make themselves busy.

'You told me to dress for ecstatic dancing,' I say.

'Well done, darling,' Mummy seems pleased with my pleather and zebra print combination. I've even managed to fashion a headband.

'You look like,' Heather has *Sadie* on the tip of her tongue.

'You look a bit like your old school friend, Cassandra. Is she your friend again now that the *misunderstanding* about your young man has been cleared up?' Mummy insults me. Still, at least I received a few seconds of joy when she told me *well done*.

'You know Tristan's been released, don't you?' Heather says, and Mummy widens her eyes.

'Home from working away?' Mummy says

loudly enough for the Sparks to hear at the top of their estate. Never let it be known that Jacquetta's name has been spoken in the same sentence as a crook.

'Are you joining us today, Mummy?' I change the subject.

'No, I must supervise the workmen. Patrice dropped our missing keys into the gutter from out of the window... You are getting along with your young man, aren't you?' Mummy has no problem discussing my private and confidential details within earshot.

'Yes.' I answer as I climb into Heather's car.

'Why does Mummy keep asking me if I'm getting on with Ben?' I ask Heather as we start our incline to Pendle.

'It's obvious, isn't it? She doesn't... *we* don't want you to end up... like last time.' Heather keeps her eyes on the road (behind her rose-coloured spectacles).

'Mummy gets a lot of work done on her house, doesn't she?' I change the subject again, this time with a conspiratorial tease of our mother.

'Right,' Heather lets out a heavy sigh. 'I'm going to tell you something now, Pippa.'

I inhale sharply. I can tell Heather's eyes are sparkling hazel, even though they are glued to the road.

'Do you remember when Daddy's wife died?'

Heather says. I pause to work out who Heather means (such is Jacquetta's long list of suitors).

'*Your* dad's wife?' As far as I know, my own father never remarried (wherever he is).

'India, yes,' Heather says. My face drops; what is Heather going to say? I was only just thinking about Aunt India. Mummy always told me to call her *Aunt* India, always. 'Well, the night she was run over by that drunk driver, India was on her way home from Mummy's house.'

Shit. What does Heather mean? Sadie said that Aunt India was out that night to warn me against a poor choice of love match. My heart thuds against my chest as though it will break my ribs. I hope Heather can't hear it; she has just risked a glance in my direction.

'Stop fidgeting, Pippa.' Heather concentrates on joining the motorway. 'Anyway, Mummy blames herself.'

'What... I thought Tristan ran Aunt India over?'

'He did.'

'You said a drunk driver.'

'He was, Pippa. He was as drunk as the day is long when he left the pub that night. And it wasn't the first time that he'd been arrested for it. That's why he got a custodial sentence and left Cassandra, as hideous as she is, poor thing, home alone with two children under three.'

'Under two,' I correct Heather.

'Yes, whatever. I forget you were friends with her,' Heather says.

I've been trying to forget about Cassandra, but now this. Tristan was drunk? I knew he had been drinking that night, but driving when over the limit? I remember that night being very intense, and Tristan had fervently... What? What exactly did Tristan say before he left The Peacock that night? I've wasted too much of my life thinking about it, so much time forgetting that I can't remember. I know he felt guilty about the children. I understood because guilt is my go-to emotion.

'Pippa, are you listening? I'm trying to tell you about Jacquetta,' Heather continues. 'If Mummy hadn't had a crisis of confidence, if she hadn't asked for her help that night, then India would still be alive.'

And if I hadn't seduced Tristan, he wouldn't have been out drink driving. 'Aunt India walked along the road with no lighting... and she only had one eye...' I repeat Sadie's *such is life.*

'Pippa!' Heather disapproves. 'Although, that is how Mummy's compulsion started. First, she arranged for outside lighting at her house, and then the old oak trees outside the pub got a makeover. But then, she received one of those random anonymous letters from a local religious maniac, promising eternal life if she rids herself of wickedness. You know the rest.'

'Maybe Aunt India should have visited

Mummy during the day,' I say. Why haven't I had a promise in a letter? I'm not wicked. None of this is my fault.

'Mummy needed to see her urgently. It was a full moon,' Heather shakes her head.

'What do you mean?' I have never heard of urgent astrology.

'It was a full moon, quite a bright night, but by the time India left Jacquetta's house, it had clouded over. And in any case, Tristan should not have been driving in that state. Poor Mummy couldn't find her keys, which was the main reason India visited. Jacquetta panicked and couldn't remember what India had advised her to do. I know you came out when the ambulance arrived, but, well, we both know it was too late. Mummy still feels guilty today, and it wasn't her fault. I know she won't have said anything to you because you were there. She thinks you were traumatised.'

'I was,' I say. I was traumatised for a slightly different reason.

'I know, Pippa. It must have been awful for you, and I'm sorry if I ever...' Heather hesitates. 'I know the truth, don't worry.'

Shit.

'Are you alright?' Heather is looking for a parking space suitably big enough for her car. 'I hope you're not feeling off-kilter again. I know the truth about how much you were drinking, Pippa. That's why I've brought you here. I think you'll really benefit from the breathing exercises.'

'I'm fine, thank you.' Phew, Heather was talking about me drinking and feeling weird. And I thought she meant she knew the truth. I am clueless once again about Mummy's quirks. Ordering poor Aunt India (who I remember she disliked at the time) to help her find her keys on a moonlit night. I prefer today's version of Mummy, feared and pointlessly revamping her home.

As we get out of the car, I realise that I have forgotten to be anxious about today. I'm in a strange place, and I'm about to meet strange people. And as they park up alongside Heather in their matching planet loving wagons, I realise why Heather micro-managed my jalopy's carbon footprint today.

'Are you really alright?' Heather puts her head on one side, inferring, *you're not alright, are you?*

'Yes, I'm fine!' I squeal.

'No, I meant about *everything*,' Heather puts her hand on my hand as I try and free myself from the seatbelt.

'I couldn't be better!' (I wish my voice wasn't so high pitched.) 'I'm on holiday, Ben says he wants to take care of me, and my sister has treated me to a day of hippy shit.' I avoid mentioning Sadie and the kitten.

Heather actually laughed at my lampoon as though she has a sense of humour. 'I was worried about your... the thing with the cat yesterday, and you seem different. You say Ben wants to take care of you?' Heather's smile turns into a frown.

'That's what he says. Actually, he's preparing a romantic evening for us as we speak so that he can tell me his plans.'

'His plans for The Peacock?' Heather ping-pongs her eyeballs across my face.

'No...' I am cut off by a rapping knuckle on Heather's driver's door window.

'Yes, we're coming!' Heather beckons me, jumps out of her car and whispers, 'some people have got no patience.'

Chapter Twenty

Not one of Heather's retreat companions wears pleather. If smocks and shawls are dressing for dancing, then I have made a massive faux pas. I whip my zebra headband off my head and hide it tightly in the fist of my left hand while pleasantries are passed around.

Heather's long, dark hair is knotted in two plaits around her crown (I miss Sadie). I look at my watch to start the countdown; today can't last forever.

'This is my sister, Pippa. I've been trying to get her to come to this event for aaaages, but she has to work, poor thing,' Heather introduces me with a mix of pride and prejudice. The retreat buddies pull compassion out of their faces, but I read envy in their minds. I'm an independent woman who has earned her stripes at the company I work for by my own merit. It is a mere coincidence that Mr Bland fancied Jacquetta. I'm already the employed enemy today, a survivor of the established system. And I'm glad I don't have to do the school run every day. No regrets, none, no sorrow for my ever-decreasing cycle. Not even one.

The women's retreat is hosted inside an old Victorian building. Countless floors have been taken over and disfigured with fire doors and fire extinguishers (one propping the other open as is both illegal and customary). Our feet sound as though they are tap dancing as we enter the room where a circle has formed with oversized cushions and hippy shit. My nose starts itching, and my mouth feels dry. I try my very best not to cough because footsteps are the only other sound echoing around. The room smells of incense and education.

Heather notices my throat tickle as we all sit down. I am the first to be passed a drink to quench my cough. This is not water but a spicy brew in a copper flagon, so heavy it requires two hands. I look up, and all the other women are staring at me... am I supposed to pass this around? 'Moscow mule, Pippa; don't worry, yours is without vodka.' Heather whispers, and I am relieved to notice that everyone has their own portion in similar-looking cups. I think Heather must be joking about the cocktail quality of our refreshment; it is ten in the morning. This staycation gets better and better.

After the mocktails are cleared away, a circle is formed around a conglomeration of candles. We each choose a big cushion to sit on. In front of each place setting are two tarot cards. My chance at last! I smile at Heather, and she nods in approval, indicating they are for 'after'.

A woman gives a speech about the retreat, although I'm not even listening. I wish my superpower was x-ray vision, and then I would be able to read the forbidden forecasters. Thank goodness for Heather; she nudges me in the ribs because we are about to start today's first audience participation. Another speech about the circle of life is delivered with the same amount of gusto (but without really saying anything). There is a good chance that I have closed myself off from Heather's intended unblocking. I'm like a child in front of a Christmas tree staring at these cards. We are then invited to take our turn and contribute one word to the circle.

One word each. Not our name (this is the only time in my life that I am glad to be named Epiphany, and I can't even use it). This is the way we spit something out on a weird and wonderful morning. Where I was the first to receive liquid refreshment, I am the last to take my turn in the word game. This does nothing for my nerves, and my eyes dart around for an emergency exit. I am concerned that coughing and asking to be excused would draw attention to me (still, it would be worth it).

An early contender of the circle shouts 'spiral.' Damn it, I was about to say that. The women close in with *nurture, family, contentment,* and so on. I don't have a word, and it's nearly my turn. Heather offers 'passion' (of course, she does).

I pause, and I look at how all the women are dressed with their lack of leggings or fakery. 'Wispy,' I shout and hear titters. I was only trying to fit in. This entire scenario is reminiscent of school, and I blame these dormant bricks for my outburst. I read a question in Heather: *Have you been drinking?*

Time for the enforced dancing, and Heather's words ring in my head; '*No one is forcing you to do anything, Pippa.*' I hope she wasn't lying. We are all invited to pick a partner, but it can't be someone we already know. To me, that's not *picking* because if I had my choice, Heather would be my partner. Even though she is taller than me (and therefore not ideal), Heather is better than the devil you know in this scenario. I watch her gush over an equally tall bailaora, and they shimmy over to the oversized cushions hand in hand. The leader grabs my hand because I am the only woman without a partner. This is why the room smells like school; I was always the last one chosen.

What happens next is not yoga. We touch hands and feet, we close our eyes, we cup our vulvas (I predict cupping your partner would be negatively reviewed). Hands on chests vibrate with the rhythm of lub-dub. My heart is something I never think about; it moves whether I like it or not. The lights dim, and the music starts. We dance ecstatically (whether we can or not).

This is when I start to feel strange. I feel hot, not a *Sadie* kind of hot, or an ear-burning hot. Not even a bad choice of plastic leggings hot. I am burning up... I'm frumpy, fair, and almost forty. And I think I'm having my first hot flush. I need to sit down.

The music is not the kind of vibe to sing along to. My temporary retreat buddies have their eyes closed, their feet stomping, and their arms reaching. Turned on, tuned in, and dropped out. I try to move my hips in a circular movement, the obvious choice for social lepers. I really need to sit down. No one is forcing me to do anything, but I am stopped from doing something. I can't move. My hips are heavy, my head droops forwards, and my hands drag for my knees. I can't move, but I need to sit down. I imagine myself stapled to a scarecrow's frame. Seven magpies have pecked out my eyes, and I can't move. I must sit down.

This reminds me of the time when Cassandra finished my sentence for me. Socially... socially... (I wanted to say that I was struggling in social situations) Cassandra offered up the word 'inept'. She was wrong to say it but correct in her meaning. No one is forcing me to do anything, but I am clumsy, crude, and incompetent. Without skill, I fall to the floor. I was trying to sit down, but my heavy hips beat me to it. The crows will consume the crop because of my failed decoy. Sabotage of sun reaching, rooted verdure is an enemy to the familiar. I pretend to be fine, 'I just needed to sit down,' I say over the trance. No one can hear me. No one is listening. I am rooted in the ground.

The music stops, and the lights are flipped. Looking out of the window, I notice a building opposite, a potential viewpoint providing the answer to the question, the missing piece of the puzzle. What must society do with women when they have passed childbearing age? Step up to this aperture and observe menopausal jerking stapled to a frame. Roll out the stocks and pillory; the witches are here, and one of them has prematurely completed her decline. We will celebrate her social ineptitude with public humiliation... She's reached halfway, but she's already there... I wonder when she's going to have an epiphany... It's happening whether she likes it or not.

I know I have landed on my claimed cushion because Heather arrives next to me, and she never gets things wrong. With all the movement and ecstasy, I appear to have lost one of my anticipated tarot cards. The candles remain lit in the centre; they are supposed to be hot; I am supposed to moderate. Heather passes me a drink, which I down in one. Finally, I am allowed to flip the switch. My single tarot card is The Three of Cups. I read about a period of great happiness and abundance, positive feelings towards three significant people in my life... Also, reuniting with a long, lost relative.

'That's a good card,' says Heather.

'I've only got one card,' I look around for my missing fortune.

'Maybe you only asked one question.' Heather carries a gentle tone sitting beside me, and I don't believe it.

'What did your reading say?'

'I didn't turn mine over; I don't need them, Pipsqueak.'

I open my mouth to say something, but I am stopped by further instruction. It is time to breathe, and once again, the lights are dimmed. How theatrical.

Now I can't close my mouth. I'm not allowed; all mouths are open inside this circle. Shoulder blades and backs of skulls knock against the hardwood floor. I am insulated beneath, yet I feel the sensation of marbles landing on tiles. I think I preferred Mummy's non-alcoholic afternoon tea.

Facing the high ceiling catching flies feels unnatural. Another kind of trance-inducing music fills my ears. It sounds like pipes and mermaids, and I sound like snorting and drooling. 'Get out of your head and control your breathing.' Hands press down on my already rooted shoulders. My two weeks' holiday is wasted on confusion; I've just been told to stop thinking but concentrate.

Heather's leader must know what she's doing because once I am free to secretly close my mouth and turn my head to the side; I drift off and try to do what I have craved to do for years. As my mind switches off, I realise I am half asleep. This is where the intrusion begins, and I start to smell chlorine.

I had never been in a fight. Not really.

Heather used to sit on me if she viewed I had done something wrong. It was cold and frosty at swim class. Cassandra wore a royal blue, houndstooth cossie she boasted had arrived from her aunt's generosity. At the time, this was the height of fashion (for a middle-aged woman, not for an eleven-year-old child). I wore Heather's hand me down, where modesty ruled over style. I can't remember what we were arguing about... something to do with how to sing the mulberry bush rhyme. Although I am back there now, I am conscious of the irony that I am going round the mulberry bush in a circle of meditating menopausal matriarchs.

Cassandra gripped my forearms, gaining purchase at the elbow. I grabbed her (how dare I?). It was obvious who would get the upper hand. Without warning, she shoved me so forcefully with the strength of her premature upper-body broadness that I fell backwards onto the wet tiles. My teeth rattled inside my face forming instant tears, the appearance of which produced an involuntary laugh. And the memory of this is why I grit my teeth at night. I looked up to see Sadie, the girl from the *can't swim* group looking all concerned with wide hazel eyes offset against her dark hair. The other girls crowded around the pusher, asking Cassandra if SHE was alright... Goodness knows why I stayed friends with her and asked her if she was 'alright' for so many years. Off I was banished to the drowning group, we were the same but different, and Sadie never seemed to care that she couldn't swim. There we drowned round the mulberry bush because floating proved us guilty (except we didn't drown because the swim teacher ridiculed us).

I think I preferred to take my chances on the ducking stool. I'm frumpy, fair, almost forty, and I've just had an epiphany. I know what my family are, and it hurts that they kept it from me.

Jacquetta was desperate to see India on the night of a full moon because she had a crisis of confidence? Held Mr Bland in transfixion all these years so that I keep my job of sums? Raising spirits to help her with the key problem? She didn't realise how strong her powers were when she helped the woman at afternoon tea redress her balance.

Heather spells a bumper crop every year in her hocus pocus garden of potent plants and herbs. She believes magic is divined by hanging glass bottles from trees.

Cassandra claims to be related to me, a distant cousin or something to do with Aunt India (not my blood relative but part of the nest of vipers).

Tristan was not magnetised to me. It was the other way round. Bewitched and held in a grandiose state of denial, thinking Tristan wanted me kept me happy and kept me at The Peacock. I begged until he told me to stop. I remember that night, 'You're coming on to me too strong, Pippa. You've got to stop it,' Tristan shouted in my face until he left and killed India. This was the way he drove his car, drunk and around the corner. I carried on drinking. Drinking and thinking I was gorgeous, looking in the mirror and seeing what I wanted to see. Until I convinced myself that every-thing was my fault and hid away like a faulty, fault, and nearly faulty.

Sadie is the only normal one (I miss Sadie).

I've served my purpose, done my time, and suddenly need a lease to live in my home. Every-thing I touch in that flat breaks, and I didn't even manage to raise a feline. Ben will take care of it; Ben wants to take care of me.

It is only because my stomach starts to cramp that I realise the music stopped a while ago. The lights are on again, and the woman has stopped going round with a soft and artificial feather.

'Are you alright, Pippa?'

I really try to answer. I want to form words to explain the crippling abdominal pain twisting my guts like a slithering nest of vipers. I want to wait for the explanation of static hips rooted to the spot, unblocking and celebrating my womanhood.

'She's fine, aren't you, Pippa?' Heather butts in. She and the other retreat buddies appear un-affected by the spell. Here we go round my mul-berry bush, unaware of my strength.

'Heather was just telling us about the amazing visualisation she had during breathing,' Heather's leader says. I'm still on the floor in a weird and waking night-nurse paralysis.

'My garden was like an orchard filled with a bounteous and beautiful crop. And as the first apple fell into my hand, I saw my husband's face in the blush.'

Of course, it did; Heather's hallucination was about fertile apples. Of course, it was; only she was not meditating. She was thinking about what she would do next in her garden. Making lists in her head instead of concentrating on breathing; 'collect the apples, shag the husband,' and so on. Heather's house and garden are not your average. Her lawn is measured in acreage and would be advertised as a smallholding if she and Rhys ever decide to sell. I'm sure it was Heather wailing at the side of me during the breathing. I wish I could howl. My insides are in knots.

The circle performs a wispy round of applause for Heather's greatness. I am starting to come round from a deep state of spiritual trance. My extremities and my throat start to tingle. Is this anger? I manage to move my left shoulder blade, and I feel the sticky unpeeling of a plastic-coated card. This must be my missing tarot. I shut my eyes and read 'The Fool' representing folly and intoxication.

'I don't think your sister's alright, you know,' the voice of a buddy comes in sideways.

'Are you alright, Pippa?' Heather speaks to me as though I'm hard of hearing. Can't she see how much pain I'm in?

'I've seen this before. I think she's got that

thing where you're awake and asleep at the same time. It happened to Penelope at the conscious reading event.' The buddy says.

I really want to laugh, but my face is frozen. Once I defrost, I shall laugh long and loud at *conscious reading*. I know what she meant, but mischief is playing with my mind.

'Let's try and help her to sit up.'

'I'll bring her some water.'

I want to ask for more Moscow mule, but I am unable because I'm rooted to the spot.

I am propped up like a doll. Water is offered and douses my front. The mechanics of my diaphragm kick me in the middle, and I can speak again but only just. 'Cramp,' I blurt out.

'Cramp?' Heather asks. I point at my stomach and widen my eyes.

'That's good!' The leader says. 'It means the meditation got through to her womanhood.'

'Well done, Pippa,' Heather congratulates me for my crippling pain. I can't move and wonder what will happen if I need to use the facilities. How will I get home? Is this where I live now? Opiates are produced from inside a canvas bag belonging to a retreat buddy. My catatonia deepens.

As ripped as she is, Heather struggles to carry me down the stairs. My feet flap around at the bottom of my legs like a French marionette's. Only when we reach the fresh air, she concludes I am 'Acting weird again, Pippa.' We are slightly out of earshot of the other women. They all agree it is a great shame that Heather and I are unable to join in further female bonding (because of my waxy flexibility). Buckled in the front passenger seat of Heather's eco-wagon, I shut my eyes, and we begin the descent to The Peacock.

Chapter Twenty-One

'She's always had a delicate constitution.'
'*Very* sensitive.'
Heather and Mummy are out on the front driveway discussing my condition.

'What did they give her?'

'I didn't see, but it could only have been an over-the-counter painkiller. Anyway, that building is hot because it's haunted. Bound to be, it used to be a school.'

I want to tell Heather that we both know my performance began before I was resurrected, but I'm still trapped in the front seat of Heather's car.

'I thought you said the retreat would sweep negativity away?' Mummy asks Heather.

'Listen, Jacquetta. First of all, they are all vegan in the women's group. And Pippa strolled in looking like a walking nightmare for PETA.'

'Oh,' Mummy says. She had a bird's nest removed from one of The Peacock's trees while we were out. Why am I being judged?

'And she was wailing during the breathing. Howling as though she was bottom of the pile at the workhouse,' Heather shakes her head. I thought *she* was making the wailing noise not me.

'That will be her heritage, on her father's side,' Jacquetta says. 'What card did she get?'

'The Three of Cups.'

'Everyone gets the abundance card; it's a con, Heather. Not everyone can be abundant.'

'Yes, we can, Mother.' Heather only addresses Mummy with a proper noun when she wishes to correct her. Everyone has the right to be abundant.

I see the front entrance of The Peacock opening. Ben is saying goodbye to a visitor. Ben asked me what time I would be home so that he could take care of any and all trace of plotting and planning by the time I returned. I know what my family are now I just don't know what this means for me.

I see Ben saying goodbye to Tristan at the front of The Peacock. Tristan? Does that mean Cassandra has been here too? Heather waves and promises to wait for their offer.

I miss Sadie.

I knew Heather was in on it. Had Ben asked her to get rid of me for the day and render me useless? Or was Ben waiting for me to leave the premises so that he could invite all kinds to unlock my defences? I have lived in the flat above The Peacock for as long as I can remember.

'Should I fetch John to help push her out of your car?' Mummy looks down on me as though I am a sack of potatoes bought on special offer, too big to not go to waste.

'It's alright, Jacquetta. I think I can manage

to prize her out of the front seat.' Heather dashes around to the passenger side and starts pulling my legs out onto Mummy's driveway, one foot at a time.

'Hang on, let me take care of it,' Ben has rushed over to help. Not me, it. 'Are you alright, Pippa?'

'She can't hear you; she's been comatose since the ecstatic dancing,' Heather talks about me, and Ben gently moves hair out of my eyes.

'Did you give her something to drink? You know it doesn't agree with her,' Ben says.

'No. *I* didn't see Pippa drinking anything... we were at a women's retreat, Ben. What did you think we were doing?' Heather looks at her feet. 'Someone gave her a painkiller because she had a stomach ache.'

Ben gave Heather a dismissive look, reaches into the car, lifts me out, and carries me towards The Peacock. He's taking care of it. Ben turns back to Heather and Mummy. 'I'll let her sleep it off, and then I'll tell her what we've agreed. It's only fair.'

'Do you think that's wise? She's not going to like it when she finds out.' Heather thinks I can't hear.

'I've got to tell her! It's her home. Pippa, are you awake?' Ben looks down on me, and I am surprised his face is so caring.

'Are you absolutely sure that you're able to move forwards with this, Ben?' Heather says.

'I'm going to get John!' Mummy wails.

'I don't think this is the time or place to discuss it. Like I said, I think Pippa should know the truth first. Hang on; I think she's coming round.' Ben is so strong that he can conduct a conversation with Mummy and Heather while holding up my limp limbs and loosely hanging head.

Mummy and Heather watch Ben carry me all the way to the entrance of The Peacock as though this is the last time they will ever see me.

Back in my flat, Ben carefully lays me on the rug and places a soft cushion under my head. I lie on my back, waiting for him to take care of me. Ben said it plenty of times. The more he said it, the more I heard the threat in his words. I'll take care of you. Not I *can* take care of you, but I'll take care of you. I'll take care of it. I'll take care of you and get rid of the body. Not your body, the body.

Ben feels my forehead with the back of his hand. I am so weak that I can't read his mind. Is he measuring my forehead and comparing me to Cassandra? Why was Tristan here? Was he sharing info about me with Ben?

Ben returns with a glass of clear liquid. He sits me up and holds me upright with his knee. 'Try and drink something, Pippa, please,' he whispers. I open my mouth to speak, but the cold glass clashes against my teeth. 'Sorry, here, try and sip then.'

I sit with my mouth open. Ben patiently crouches beside me for longer than is comfortable. Eventually, he puts the glass on the table, and my heavy body does not fall back onto the temporary day bed as I thought it would. I am trapped in the position Ben fixed me in, sitting upright with my legs in front of me. All I need now is Aunt India's grimoire in the hope that it falls open on the page with Jacquetta and Heather's faces. Their photograph included a fantastic fact about broomsticks. I could show Ben that I know what's going on. I know what my family is, and I know he knows I know.

'Look, Pippa, I don't know what's going on. Do you need a doctor?' Ben runs his hand through his dark, dark hair. 'Can you blink? One blink for yes...'

My eyelids perform an involuntary flutter. I don't need a doctor, but I do need to close my mouth. Ben knows this too; he massages the side of my face until my jaw springs backwards like the end of a yawn. The complex manipulation of my nervous system stimulates me out of stupor but not quickly enough. Ben needs to tell me the truth; it's only fair. 'Those two nights I stayed at Cassandra's, I had an epiphany.'

Is he fucking joking?

'I realised that you are my future, Pippa. I love you, and I want to take care of you.' As Ben speaks, my eyelids start flickering again. This must be what Heather and Mummy mean by *being weird*. Does Ben want to put me out of my misery? That loving me means he can't watch me suffer in the trapping transfixion that Mummy holds me in? 'Don't say no, Pippa,' Ben rubs the side of my face a little more furiously. This will take ages to kill me (if it ever does). 'At first, I thought about you and me moving away from here, given the location.'

What's wrong with the location, I wonder?

'I did have a poke about, but the job situation is looking dire after lockdown. You must realise that, Pippa?' Ben darts his head, intensely looking into my eyes. I don't flicker. 'So, when this opportunity came up, it seemed too good to miss. And I know it's not ideal, but Cass and Tristan only want to be silent partners. Cassandra doesn't want Tristan anywhere near the place, given his... you know.'

Yes, I know; I know that I made a fool of myself. This must be why I'm trapped in stocks and pillories, suffering the humiliation of Ben knowing what I did, how I held Tristan with wrathful obsession. None of which was my fault; erotomania is a rare delusion.

'Basically, he promised to sign up for help from the alcohol dependency service. I don't know the full court restrictions, but it doesn't include stumping up the money to reopen The Peacock. He just can't come in here once it is open, and he won't. Not with Cassandra watching him.'

Not with those nostrils.

Eventually, Ben decides to put me to bed. I watch him with dry eyes. He picks me up; he puts me down. This is the way we get undressed on a cold and frosty evening. He takes my clothes off;

he dresses me in pyjamas. I'm all dressed up and ready for bed (I prefer Sadie's makeover). Ben realises I might need to attend to the necessary, and he seats me in the bathroom. He closes the door (I miss Sadie).

Ben even tries to tease my mouth open with a wet flannel, telling me I must drink something; otherwise, he will have to take me to see my GP. I know that dehydration won't kill me; I've done it before, many times. At least the stomach cramps have stopped, or maybe they're still going on underneath this veil of paralysis that Heather has put me under. No doubt she'll release me once a rushed deal has been struck amongst the nest of vipers. This doesn't seem enough time to see me off for want of water.

It's only fair that I know the truth, but I'm unable to defend myself because neurosis has rooted me to the spot. Sadie would know what to do if she was here. Sadie would tell them she doesn't agree; I don't agree. Over my dead body are Cassandra and Tristan taking over Mummy's pub.

My boyfriend plans to smother me in my sleep.

Ben goes on to tell me the ins and outs of his plan. This must have been what he had in mind for our romantic evening (as I am seated on the floor, I cannot see the imaginary dinner). 'Your father must have been a very clever man, Pippa.' Ben has met John. He knows John is not my father (and he definitely didn't mean Maddox, no one has heard hide nor hair of him for as long as I can remember). 'He bought the building; The Peacock is a freehold!' Ben has a massive grin on his face. I need to set him straight; this is Mummy's pub. 'Apparently your mum's mates named themselves The Wildes... They all bought the pub together, meaning there is no brewery interference. Cass told me that your mother and father, Heather's dad and his wife, and John knew one another from as far back as anyone can remember. *And* Cass inherited a share because your aunt was her godmother. That's what she is, some distant coven of your aunt's, so you're not really related.' Ben said coven instead of cousin, I'm sure of it.

How does Cassandra know this? How did Cassandra get a houndstooth swimming costume and a share of The Peacock? How am I the ignorant one? This is what I'm going to die of... gaslighting. 'And the best bit is you'll get the biggest share, Pippa. Your dad's share, half your mum's share, and you and Heather get half of John's share. Heather gets half your mum's share but not all of Oswald's... it's been very complicated apparently because one of The Wildes has been missing for over seven years. But your mum, Oswald and John want to retire. Now that lockdown is over, they're giving up the pub. We just need some cash to refurb and reopen it.' Ben turns the corners of his mouth upwards and breathes air out of his nose. He is relieved that

The Peacock's complications are over. I am ever more confused, and my brain is sure to switch off under this pressure. *Be careful what you wish for*.

No wonder Ben had an epiphany; I'd love me if I thought I was about to inherit The Peacock.

Chapter Twenty-Two

Peacocks are symbolic of sexuality, spirituality, and pride. This is the way I blow my mind on a cold and frosty morning.

I woke during the witching hour, and it was only when I poured myself a glass of water that I realised I could move again. This is the first time in my life that I've been grateful for my tickling cough because that is what woke me.

I have lived in the flat above The Peacock for as long as I can remember. I was about seventeen years old when I made my way across Mummy's moat; living under her roof but not living at home was an offer too good to refuse. Without knowing the details of my tenancy, I've hidden up here until I am frumpy, fair, and almost forty. I'm still alive, though; Ben has not succeeded to take care of me. I suppose it wouldn't be fair on all the other men if he could make popcorn *and* be a murderer.

'Oh my God, you're up!' Ben's eyes squint in the warm, white halogen light. His hand is down his boxer shorts; he's still half asleep. My mind allows an intrusion about Ben's proposition. If I sink, I'll drown in Cassandra's spirits, and if I swim, my guilt shall imprison me up here. Here we go round The Peacock's licence with post-pandemic innovation. I haven't minded being trapped so far, but that was under Mummy's rule. I wonder if Ben will employ Grace Poole to nurse me, red-headed, plain, and unappealing. 'Pippa, are you alright? I was worried about you before. You were acting...'

'Weird...' I cough. I wasn't acting, though; none of this is my fault.

'Oh,' Ben laughs a cosseting laugh and hugs me to his bare chest. I smell success and biscuits. 'Do you want a cup of tea as well as your water?'

I don't answer; I'm too busy drinking.

'Let's go back to bed, Pippa,' Ben leads me back to the bedroom, and I follow him without a quibble.

Another seventy-two hours have passed without reading anything, not even an Agatha Christie. I really am not acting my usual self. The past seventy-two hours drained me, and I fall asleep, although not as deeply as I'd like.

It feels like Ben has turned me over, I lie on my front, and my breath is shallow. I hear Ben talking in his sleep; I feel the pillow next to my face. I am smothered in mint, apple, and cloves. I scream with as much ferocity as a horror movie fan: long, loud, and sudden. 'What the hell is going on?' Ben wakes with a start. 'Are you alright, Pippa? Did you have a nightmare?'

I switch the light on and look under the covers and down both sides of the bed. 'I thought I saw Sadie in the mirror,' I shout. Ben takes my half-asleep intrusion as a thing I feared and holds me close to his digestive smelling chest.

'There's no one here but you and me,' Ben softens his tone, although I have woken him twice tonight. 'Go back to sleep, Pippa. I agree there are too many mirrors in this bedroom, though.'

How did Ben know I don't like the mirrors?

If India Kitten was taken away from me by some hanging-bottle-key-turning incantation, then it is only fair that I reclaim her. She is rightfully mine, and Sadie gave her to me. Thankfully, paralysis has not returned, but I still haven't had enough sleep when I wake again. I leave The Peacock, and although it is months since everything reopened, dawn has not yet appeared.

The kitty carrier bangs against my legs without punishment. When India Kitten finds me this time, she won't want to leave me again. Especially as I've just decided she is a house cat. We will be together in aloof harmony. Ben's antihistamine compromise is exchanged for ownership of The Peacock. India Kitten is worth it. When I reach the top of the estate in my incognito big boots and winter coat, I see lights on inside the Sparks' house.

Shit. They're not meant to be awake yet... The Sparks' front door opens, and the car on the driveway lights up its headlamps with key-operated magic found on modern cars (I'm used to the jalopy, central locking is a foreign luxury to me).

Mr Sparks is setting off for work. He notices me standing on his front driveway and jumps out of his skin. Then he squints his eyes in recognition.

'Hello there, are you alright?' Mr Sparks says (too loudly, I fear, for his neighbours. He must be an errant shift worker).

At first, I don't answer because I don't know how to be. I must remember I've had an epiphany, and I am on a mission to get what is rightfully mine. I'm everything to everyone and put Jacquetta on. 'Oh, hello there; I'm sorry to trouble you, Mr Sparks.' I read that he needs to set off for work; he doesn't want to keep the prior shift workers waiting. 'I wondered if I may call on India Kitten. I did promise your wife I would return.'

Mr Sparks looks at my kitty carrier and raises his eyebrows. 'Not at the moment, love, it's six in the morning. I'm only up because I work shifts.' Mr Sparks looks at his watch for extra proof. I look awkward.

If Mr Sparks loves his job so much, why doesn't he just go there? We have reached an impasse. He is waiting for me to leave, and I am waiting for him to invite me back later.

'I shall call back this afternoon, then.' I am doing an excellent Jacquetta; I'm not even wearing lipstick, and my teeth are stretched across my lips.

'If you like, love; do me a favour though, leave the cat box at home.' Mr Sparks chuckles as he talks; I suppose this is an enduring quality; though I suspect it means Mrs Sparks cannot take him seriously. The conversation is over (as far as I'm concerned). As I turn and amble away, I feel Mr Sparks' eyes boring into my back. All I can do is keep walking, and upon hearing his car drive away, I shall return.

I turn right on the estate of boxes down what they call a ginnel, a narrow passageway for dog walkers and burglars. I have no idea where this one leads. It could be like Mummy's circular corridor on the upstairs landing. Here we go round suburbia, and the first thing I see is a pair of cat's eyes staring at me. It is not India Kitten; it is Mr Sparks' car. (Tell him it's a shortcut; just tell him it's a shortcut.)

'I was just thinking, love; I'm passing The Peacock. Jump in; I'll give you a lift.' Mr Sparks speaks to me through his open car window. He sounds sinister, yet I suppose he thinks himself harmless. I know where he lives (with my cat). I've met his wife, and they've met Heather (woe betide those who cross Heather). I read pity in his mind, pity and debate. Should he leave me to wander the streets and risk my return? Or should he offer me a lift, a man on his own in a car with a passing female acquaintance? The third option is to follow me home (also known as kerb-crawling), and Mr Sparks is not the type. He has decided he can't trust me, and so have I.

'I'm fine, thank you. I can walk,' I say.

'Are you sure, love? You look a bit lost; the path I've just seen you walk out from doesn't go anywhere.'

'It's a shortcut, Mr Sparks, yes, it used to be a shortcut to The Peacock, until all of this concrete bastardised the countryside.' My hand performs a contemptuous wave (these houses were in their infancy the year I was born, but Jacquetta swears the green verdure around The Peacock was ruined).

'OK then, see you later,' Mr Sparks gives up trying to abduct me, and I postpone my mission to bring India Kitten home. No matter, he did say *see you later*. Obviously, this means I am welcome to call at his home this evening to see the cat (and steal her when their backs are turned). I venture back down the ginnel (it *doesn't* go anywhere apart from where it started...but I shan't be proved wrong). I hear Mr Sparks drive away; I wonder if he is known for his tardiness. Unreliability is not a trait well favoured in the current climate. Ben must have thought all his Christmases had come at once when he found out The Peacock was up for grabs; it is impossible to be late for work if you live on the premises.

Eventually, I reach the home stretch with my empty kitty carrier. In the distance, I notice the lights on in the upstairs windows of The Peacock. All that messing about with shortcuts took too long; I should've accepted Mr Sparks' lift, (although I may have ended up in the boot of his car). I am yet to disconfirm my cloak making suspicions as I've failed to actually *see* India Kitten alive. Goodness knows what would've happened had I stepped into that luxury saloon.

Dawn disappeared with sunrise; I have arrived home later than I anticipated. Walking up the driveway, I notice someone moving about in my bedroom... It is Sadie.

I *knew* I'd seen Sadie the second time I woke up; it wasn't a dozy intrusion. Sadie is real. She is really getting dressed in my bedroom. She is real and in my bedroom with Ben, my boyfriend, who has forsaken me again.

My pace quickens on the driveway. I can't believe Sadie has done this to me. She stroked my head when I was forlorn, and she picked passages from that fucking book of facts. She was there for me.

Ben opens the front door of The Peacock. How does one confront their lover whom they saw a moment ago with a woman and her reflection? We swap places when I try to push him out of the way.

'No hello?' Ben grabs me by the inside of my elbows. 'Where have you been? Pippa, I've been worried sick about you after yesterday... and you were so restless last night.'

'I suppose Sadie was just helping you look for me, was she?' I spit my words with venom, but I sound unstable.

'What are you talking about?' said Ben. He looks cold on the driveway in his bare feet (he should've worn bedroom slippers).

'I'm talking about Sadie, Ben. I just saw her in

the bedroom; you're not going to tell me you don't know what I'm talking about.' I need to get Sadie's version of events. How long was I gone? Ben must have laid in wait for me to leave, before springing his rendezvous into action. Sadie made out she didn't like Ben; what was someone *like me* doing with someone *like him*? Was she pulling the wool over my eyes? Has everyone lied to me?

Sadie was the only person I could trust in this midsummer night's dream. Before I saw her in my bedroom with stupid Ben, I wanted to ask what she makes of the pub takeover. Would Sadie think I'm being taken for a fool? Can Cassandra keep her husband (and herself) away from The Peacock? Does Ben really love me, or am I still a convenience (with a large inheritance)?

Could Sadie be a succubus? Bewitching me with apples and sucking the life out of Ben (I should have given her feet a closer inspection). Is Sadie *one of them* trysting around the mulberry bush with Mummy and my sister? I scramble to the door and shut Ben out. Half naked on the driveway, he bangs his fist and shouts accusations; have I lost my mind? He whispers utterances of unfairness; he is *freezing to death* out there. I turn to guard the entrance using my gluteus muscle until I hear him capitulate. He *will* cross the road to seek advice from my mother in his *bare feet* (which is *ridiculous*).

I bolt the locks behind me, and I hear a voice. 'I'm down here, Pippa.'

'What the hell do you think you're doing?' I scream at Sadie. She is wearing her trademark shiny pants, and she's as drunk as a lord.

'Sitting on the floor of a pub that I've been banished from, Pippa.' Sadie is untroubled by my tone, and as much as I want to find out if what I saw at the window really happened, Sadie has just touched on our inheritance-in-common. She's not banished; she's here.

'I meant, what were you doing with my boyfriend?'

Sadie puts a voice on to mimic me, *'my boyfriend'*.

'Have you been drinking, Sadie?' I already know the answer.

'I've been drinking all night long, Pippa. There's no shame in it. I just haven't been to bed yet, and neither have you!' Sadie points at me (rather successfully, considering the state she's in).

'I have. I just went out to find...' I look at the empty kitty carrier (she is in no state to hear about the catnapping).

'And I just went to find you, Pippa. In your bed, but you weren't there, just that stupid Ben. You keep Mum's *Book of Fantastic Facts* by your pillow...' Sadie sounds about ten years old.

We have been using Aunt India's gift as a doorstop. Ben started it; I would never normally mistreat a book… I must never tell Sadie, especially as I managed to lose her gifted cat.

'So, you didn't sleep with him then?' I already know the answer, but it is only fair to check Sadie's alibi as I had confronted Ben outside.

'I didn't sleep with him. You did, though,' Sadie sighed. 'And last I heard Ben *needed to talk.*'

How things have changed since I last saw Sadie, seventy-two hours ago.

'He said he had an epiphany, and he loves me.' As I hear my words, I think I sound gullible.

'Oh, he's had an Epiphany alright; he's had you like a dog has its dinner. I thought he didn't know your full name?' Sadie remembers everything, and her figurative words worry me. Do not get onto the subject of pets, Pippa. Just change the subject.

'Ben wants to take over the pub.'

'I bet he fucking does.' Sadie stands and walks behind the bar. She knows where everything is and pours herself a drink. 'Oswald has written me out.'

'Your dad?' I ask.

'Yes, and that fucking Cassandra is getting my share; Cassandra and our sister-in-common, the green goddess.' Sadie offers me a sip of her drink.

'I could give you part of my share, Sadie. I'm getting Mummy and Daddy's bit and half of John's, according to Ben.' Now I'm the one who sounds ten years old, my father's name is on the tip of my tongue, I *never* referred to him as Daddy.

'*According to Ben,*' Sadie mimics me again. 'Ben's playing you for a fool, Pippa. Can't you see that? Just like fucking Cassandra, she had Mum wrapped around her little finger when I was growing up.'

'She does that,' I say in a small voice.

'Yeah, well, Cassandra was the daughter of Mum's distant cousin who got under Mum's skin and made her feel guilty for ensnaring Oswald. She tried to say that Cassandra was dad's child.'

I imagine Cassandra as my half-sister's half-sister, and my thoughts float away to swim class and houndstooth. Sadie is still talking to herself like Miss Flite.

'Then Cassandra's mother found out she was ill and begged Mum to look after Cassandra when she died. Mum immediately took on the role of godmother, but it was a long and cruel illness, and Cassandra played my mother like a fiddle during her own mother's dying years. Changing her hair to look like me, copying my clothes. Cassandra even took Tristan off me. All the while, India thought she was the perfect daughter.'

I sort of know all of this. I remember Cassandra's mother dying just after her eighteenth birthday, and she was always skilled in the dark art of enchantment. When we were younger, Heather always teased me for copying Cassandra. It is satisfying to think that Cassandra wanted to be Sadie.

'That's why I always liked you so much, Pippa. With your hair, you could only be yourself,' Sadie smiles.

'Oscar Wilde said that,' I love how Sadie is fluent in literary passages and quotes.

'Be yourself because Sadie is taken.' Sadie points at me with her glass in her hand.

'Is that why they banished you?' I have no recollection of Sadie being asked to leave. No wonder this is a touchy subject if India chose Cassandra over her own daughter. I must tread carefully, Sadie is drunk, and I almost lost her by accusing her of shagging Ben.

'I had no choice to do what I did. I needed the attention.' Sadie speaks with the realisation that telling me what happened would be taking it too far. I *knew* we had something in common; secrets. 'Oswald has cut me out; he's giving Mum's share of the pub to Cassandra. And you know that I know that you know this is bad for both of us... or something.'

'Well, that's not fair. I'll ask Mummy to speak to Oswald,' I plead Sadie's case, almost forgetting my own epiphany (I must tell Sadie). 'You know, I had my own epiphany at Heather's menopause yoga.' I am planning to tell Sadie that I know what my family really are.

'Ha! You wouldn't know what to do with an epiphany...'

I forgive Sadie's defrocking; she has been very patient with me.

'No, they'll have to die. It's the only way... You'll have to do it, Pippa. First, take Heather out. She'll be easy; it'll be like blowing a dandelion clock. Then kill Cassandra.' Sadie's chest rises and falls with murderous intent. If she's so incensed, why doesn't she do it? 'What's wrong, Pippa?'

'Why do I have to kill them?' I say in my small, incredulous voice.

'Because, Pippa, you've done it before.'

Shit.

Chapter Twenty-Three

I am all things to all people when I arrive at Mummy's door. I left Sadie in my bed to sleep off her wrongdoings, and she promised to leave without being seen. No one must know of our Machiavellian scheme, and I must pretend today to be normal. It turns out I *can* be easily persuaded.

'Yes, Mummy, everything is alright,' I answer a barrage of questions thrown at me as Mummy unlocks her door that cannot be unlocked.

'You were acting weird though, Pippa,' Ben repeats like the Duracell Bunny.

'Thank you for reminding me, Ben, I must thank Heather for taking me to menopause yoga.' I sound like a fucking Stepford wife. I like my style.

'Well, that's alright then,' Mummy is appeased by my amiability.

'Hang on, Pippa. I was *really* worried about you. You could hardly talk or walk yesterday,' Ben's concern surprises me, and I thank him with a pat on the bottom (like all good wives do).

'Ah, that will be the breathing exercises she did at the women's retreat, Ben. It's powerful stuff,' Mummy talks as I expected she would (magically).

'That doesn't explain why she shoved me out of the house in my underpants!' Ben and Mummy speak as though I am not here. I don't mind.

'Well, what goes on between you two is none of my business,' Mummy changes her tune.

'Where had you been, Pippa?' Ben says.

'Hmm?' I utter, as though I know not of what Ben refers to.

'This morning, I woke up, and you were out somewhere... I was worried.'

'You were right to be worried Ben, I was sleepwalking.' I decide against mentioning India Kitten because then I would have to explain about Sadie.

'Oh, sleepwalking,' Mummy bats me away with her chiffon scarf with *'that explains everything'* dismissal.

'You were saying something about... who's that woman... that sister?' Sadie's name is on the tip of Ben's tongue. I manage to offer Ben a look that is both quizzical and condescending. I suppose this is how gaslighting plays out for the narcissist. I feel awesome. 'Oh, never mind.' Ben retreats... almost. 'I think we should go and have a lie down for a bit. Neither of us got much sleep last night... I could make us both a hot chocolate.'

'Can we watch a chick flick too?' I almost forget I'm supposed to be euthanizing my sibling.

'If you like, Pippa.' Ben pulls me into a one-armed embrace and kisses the top of my head. The poor thing must be freezing in his underwear and bare feet.

It is only as we float across the road that I

realise; Ben and I cannot return to the flat because Sadie will probably still be asleep upstairs. I must get my brain in gear. What would Lizzie Borden do?

'Ben, I would love to go to that cafe in the nature reserve. They do a lovely hot chocolate. We can get takeout cups and then come home to bed,' I am enjoying Stepford Pippa.

'Well... alright. Can I put some clothes on first, Pippa? I've been lucky no one's driven past.' Ben loves me. He must. Only a love-locked man would streak across the road with worry for his damsel. I must think quickly.

'I'll wait here,' I have no choice. If Sadie is asleep in our bed, I shall drown in mortification. If Sadie has left (unseen, as promised), then I shall swim towards our shared goal. Discovering the key in my coat pocket, I jump into the jalopy, start the engine, and drive away with purpose to my first killing. Ben must have heard me start the engine and retreats from halfway up the stairs with a sad little pair of trousers trailing between his legs.

I know the way to Heather's house, but do I know the way to homicide? How much petrol will I need? How will I do it? Will Sadie deny me if I get caught? Do I need to disguise myself? I should have scrupulously planned this act of premeditation... Hopefully, my soon-to-be legal team will pick this up and run with it. I have harboured a secret desire to stand trial for a crime of passion for a while now. Dreams *can* come true.

I start to feel hot again, and I am feared that my waking paralysis will return while in charge of the jalopy. Perhaps some music will settle me. The radio gives me the news instead. How many vaccinations does it take to be free from Covid? That sounds like a joke, and I can't focus. I must concentrate on the killing. I wish I wasn't wearing this oversized coat. I should stop to take it off and throw it on the back seat. Then I remember I am wearing my best pyjamas underneath. And stopping on a road whose only purpose is to be a highway would attract attention from fellow drivers. *Who is this woman delaying our journey with her pyjamas (that no doubt she keeps for best)? There is no reason to stop on this thoroughfare; she is obviously a crook. I must remember her face in case she is about to commit sororicide.*

Talking to myself is not helping (I miss Sadie), and I have not given her stratagem enough thought. If Heather and Cassandra were to drop dead of natural causes, would The Peacock automatically pass to Sadie? Would it? Why not? It does sound as though Oswald went a bit west with his thinking. Flipping his legacy in the air for Cassandra to catch on her plate and sprinkle with lemon and sugar. Why not kill them? Cassandra was only vaguely connected to India. And with Heather gone, there will be no one around to judge my life and lack of allure.

Without Heather, I would not be an inconvenience. I would no longer be a resemblance of how life was so much better *before* I came along. There would be no further unjust blame for being born; it's not my fault she is jealous of me. It is not my fault that Heather is so self-absorbed that she painted me as the least favourite daughter. I grew in Heather's shadow; even my flat is one of Heather's cast-offs (hence the mirrors). Oscar Wilde said nothing about borrowing. Too feared to have anything of my own I took from others; indulging in written adventures that don't belong to me. And even when I fall in love, I accuse my intended of philandering.

Interestingly, Ben was not on Sadie's hit list. This must mean that although she has proven her scorn for him, Sadie subconsciously believes Ben is right for me.

There are two types of people in this world. Narcissists and their victims, and that's why Heather must go. Ben doesn't want me to lose; Ben wants to take care of me. I conjure designs in my mind, Sadie and me running The Peacock together. Mummy will be allowed to visit occasionally if she promises not to berate me for recapturing India Kitten.

Shit, I have just realised I am driving at twenty miles per hour in a national speed limit zone. There is a queue of traffic behind me, cursing my stupidity. I wonder if they think I'm a Sunday stroller. I doubt that many will take pity on me for my reverse restriction. There I go again, worrying about what other people think of me; Heather's doing (she deserves to die). I really mean it.

I join the sensible speed stream, and I am yet to decide on my course of action. I am getting bloodthirsty, though. As I reach the roundabout, I have a thought. Why not run Heather over? As Sadie said, I've done it before (although I wasn't driving at the time). Driving my favourite weapon, spinning wheels with murderous intent (I wonder where Heather is, exactly).

This roundabout is famed as the most boring roundabout in the history of circles. I must speed up to be rid of it. I remember Heather said she belonged as soon as she arrived in Pendle. I think I have circumvented this dreary obstacle twice already. I just can't remember which exit to take. As soon as I think I've got it, I change my mind. If I'm hoping to mow Heather down, I must look for her running route. Where is one's sister most likely to jog? Round I go again, weaving in and out of traffic, the same traffic that cursed my earlier apprehension. My ears burn as I swerve from one lane to another. Damn it! The tickling sensation returns to my throat, and just when I'm trying to be me, I remember something I don't like about myself. Imagine the irony. I am on my way to bludgeon Heather, but my throat closes up, and I fatally choke on my trachea.

This cough is doing nothing for my driving. I have no choice but to hug the central island while attempting a one-handed search for the bottle of water hiding on the jalopy's floor. I can't drive while parched because my face streams with tears. This must be what a panic attack feels like; I've never had one because of avoidance. With both hands back on the steering wheel, all I can do is cough. No need to watch my manners and cover my mouth; I am alone inside the jalopy. The traffic does not agree; I hear beeping, screeching, and wailing.

What would Sadie do in this situation?

Chapter Twenty-Four

I wake in a room without mirrors. I could be still asleep, although I am conscious of a troubling thought. What did Sadie do with the envelope that Cassandra wrote Ben's name on?

If Sadie is like Mummy and Heather, then I have been hoodwinked. If I learnt anything from my day out with my sister, I was not responsible for India's death. I wasted what feels like half my life languishing in guilt for no reason. If I didn't kill India, then why should Sadie order me to...?

Shit! I sit up in the unfamiliar single bed. What have I done? Where the fuck am I? Incarcerated? I've always thought I can tough out a bit of solitary confinement but not if it wasn't my fault.

My head feels hung-over, but that doesn't make sense; I don't drink anymore. My jaws have been subject to an archaic torture device that will *not* coerce a confession. As I find my way to the bathroom without a door, I realise that my tongue has grown overnight, I can't speak, and I can't get a word in or out. I couldn't confess if I wanted to. 'What kind of witchcraft is this?' My shout is delivered with a cough and more coughs follow. Stifled and sharp, my throat constricts.

I hear sirens again.

'Hello, Epiphany.' The blurred features of a twenty-year-old woman wearing what might be a uniform float above me. I must correct her of my name. 'Don't try and move too quickly; the doctor gave you some sedation last night.'

'Pippa,' I cough (my name is the least of my worries at the moment, but I do have boundaries).

'That's it, try and sip some water. Are you able to tell me how you're feeling?' the (potential) nurse asks.

I roll my eyes towards the ceiling in thought.

'That's good; I can see your eye-rolling has eased off.'

Have I been rolling my eyes at this poor lamb?

'Sometimes, it's very rare, but occasionally people get a bad reaction to the meds.' The young woman turns out to be a 'nurse' called Diana. She talks at length, repeating herself with synonyms about how I'm feeling. I hear a story about how the nurse on the 'checks round' found me on the floor. I had to be brought back from the brink – but I shouldn't worry because it was a panic attack (must be a lie, I don't have them). I learnt all about oculogyric crisis; although I was given a minimal dose of a less potent antipsychotic, I had a re-action. Of course, I had a reaction; otherwise, there would've been little point in giving it to me. I do not remember accepting it, though.

The tickling sensation is pissing me off; as is

Diana. I start to wonder if I am suffering from a split personality syndrome because I liked her at first. Now I want to throw her out of the window. I cough in her face and shut her up; 'WHERE THE FUCK AM I?'

'Alight, Epiphany. It's OK,' Diana rests her hand on a small, plastic thing on her waistband. It looks a bit like a pager (powered by witchcraft, no doubt). 'You're in The Mary Shelley Unit.'

'Frankenstein?'

'Shh, try not to speak, Pippa; it's making your cough worse.'

I've changed my mind; I am dreaming. And I've changed my mind (again) about Diana.

'Try and drink this for me?' Diana holds a plastic cup to my lips; they don't seem to be working. I swallow a bit, but most of it drools out of my mouth. Diana gently pats my chin with a papery feeling towel. 'Feeling better?' Diana is looking intently at my eyes because they are on the roam again. This time, a man's face squashed against the square window panel in the door distracted me. 'Excuse me a minute,' Diana says. I like her, she's very polite. She cracks open the door revealing a slither of light. Diana covers this with her body and says something barely audible to the man, which I decipher as 'sit in the dayroom for me?' I must be in the night room. 'Where was I?' Diana returns her attention to me. I shrug in response because I don't honestly know where either of us is. 'Ah yes. Don't worry; the doctor is on his way to see you; he'll review your medication to see if we can bring the swelling down in your tongue. The night nurse noticed you've got a cough, that's why you're being barrier nursed. It sounds like a tickle, but the doctor might ask you to do some tests. He'll probably want to take some blood off you too.' Diana's work here is done, but I have so many questions for her.

'What tests?' After my outstanding A-level results, I completed an accountancy apprenticeship. I cannot prove this at this moment because I am no longer acquainted with the owners of that firm, but I know I have been tested enough already.

'It's nothing to worry about, Pippa. He might ask you for a sputum sample, he might listen to your chest. He might ask you to blow into a peak flow meter. Then again, the assistant practitioner might do that bit. Could I ask you to wear this for me?'

Sample, listen, and blow, otherwise known as tests. I accept the disposable face mask from Diana. 'Where is he taking my blood to?'

Diana smiles at my question. Her ears must have tuned in to my big tongue way of speaking, and she tells me not to worry (again). 'It's just for a routine full blood count.'

I imagine the doctor counting blood. I can count (I should get into that game).

All this telling me not to worry has distracted me. Motherfucker; Diana was trying to trick me. However, I must address her with the same good manners she offered me. 'WAIT!' Shit. That came out like passive hostility. 'Sorry, Diana. You're very nice, but are you real?'

'Yes, Pippa.' (She must have heard me!) 'I am a real nurse, don't let the 'mental health' bit put you off.'

Mental health? Diana leaves the room, and I rush to the open bathroom to throw up.

I wonder if I did kill Heather.

Chapter Twenty-Five

'Let me out,' I try to open the ward's door. It cannot be unlocked, and I regret dismissing Mummy's requests to the patron saint of keys. Here I go round mistakes and misunderstandings with the alienist. The softly, softly approach must be the accepted line of skulduggery in this Frankensteinian house. Dr Kershaw started off just like Diana but then told me he would *prefer* it if I didn't leave at the moment.

Before my request to abscond was refused, Dr Kershaw diagnosed me with asthma (who knew!). I have suffered in virtual silence all my life with a crippling throat tickling sensation when I could have become addicted to inhalers instead. I started thinking about Heather and how it was her fault. I was not coughing *on purpose;* choking was annoying *to me,* not her. I conclude that Heather deserves to be as flat as a pancake on the road somewhere near Pendle. Diana dutifully administers some of Dr Kershaw's antidote for my swollen tongue.

One of Diana's friends (I forget her name) helped me clean up after the bathroom incident. A change of clothes and an asthma inhaler do not make me want to stay. Especially as Dr Kershaw started asking me how much I usually drink. I read that he does not believe I'm allergic to alcohol; Dr Kershaw needs to work on his bedside manner.

Having picked up that I have been admitted into psychiatric care (by mistake), I must choose my words carefully. I shall not bring up the subject of Heather to my captors (what if she's dead? Asking if she's alive will point the finger at me). As much as I am puzzled by my body, I do not mention what happened after menopause yoga. Let them come to me with their enquiries, not the other way round. A gentle nudge in the right direction should set Dr Kershaw on the right path. 'Is it common for women in the predicament of menopause to be admitted here?'

'How old are you?' Dr Kershaw took my enquiry as a self-diagnosis and thumbs my observation chart.

'Oh, I'm frumpy, fair, and almost forty,' I attempt a flirt.

'This is not a gallstones ward, Epiphany.'

'It's Pippa, actually. I've been told that women can be perimenopausal for ten years before the actual finale. Would you suggest hormone therapy? And then I can be on my way.'

'That is true, Pippa. What symptoms do you have? Any irregular bleeding?' Dr Kershaw appears unfazed by my womanhood (what a professional).

'No! Just a few hot... thingies.' Suddenly, I am without the vocabulary required to explain myself. Dr Kershaw takes over the conversation with his questions. He concludes that my symptoms are caused by anxiety and will recommend that I am assessed by the clinical psychologist. This is hokum; Dr Kershaw assumes that I am a quivering wreck without knowing the whole story. Meaning I am going round in circles again; I have no intention of telling him the truth. If I am anxious, I shall pop a few of those calming tablets. I won't be telling a psychologist my private business, clinical or not (shame I'm allergic to alcohol).

After 'tests' in the clinic room, I continued my plea to face the music (either with Sadie or the police). I'm not allowed to keep the asthma inhaler on my person; I must ask a nurse if I feel breathless outside of the Bis in Die blast of a brown preventer. Also, the man who stared through my window earlier returned to listen to my conversation. These two inconveniences trouble my last nerve. Now Dr Kershaw has changed his tone to one of business.

'Would you like to step into this private interview room, and we can discuss your case?' Dr Kershaw can be very forceful when he wants to be. 'Diana can come too if you're worried.'

'She'll just tell me not to worry,' I say.

'Get a witness, love. Always get a witness,' Mr Nosy chips in. I realise now that his bulging eyes are not his fault. I bet they give weird sedatives out like sweeties in this place (I have never seen Mummy's eyes bulge on the helpers she swallows). Dr Kershaw and Diana intimate I should ignore my new friend and try again to cajole me into the interview room.

'Who is in charge here?' I fold my arms. Mummy has a 1950s respect for medical staff. This has passed to me, just like Heather's autocracies.

'The ward manager is in a meeting at the moment, Pippa. I'm sure he'd love to speak to you later. He's on the day shift today,' Diana sounds like she is running out of options.

After a failed attempt to lull me into a circle of trust that I don't want to be a part of, it appears the two clowns standing before me are unable to resolve our stalemate. I take a breath, and although I slightly begrudge that speaking is only possible because of Dr Kershaw's inhaler, I offer recourse. 'Very well, as it appears some mistake has been made, perhaps one option would be to discuss things in the cosy little room you have,' I gesture towards the room. Dr Kershaw and Diana appear bemused that I have taken charge of the situation. I imagine it is difficult to let go of control, considering how hard they must have worked during the pandemic.

Once seated in the interview room, I realise it's not as cosy as I thought; panic buttons adorn the wall reminding us of where we are. It smells of nicotine and the great unwashed.

'This isn't the first time you've asked to go home, Pippa,' Dr Kershaw starts us off.

'Can you remember anything about how you got here?' Diana is a little more concise this time.

She thinks she is reminding me, but instead, she spouts brand new information. I listen to her story about the police taking me to a place of safety when they found the jalopy on the central island of a roundabout near Pendle. There I went round the roundabout until I ran out of petrol. I think there may have been more to it than that, but I sense that Diana has been warned before by Dr Kershaw for beating around the bush. Dr Kershaw takes over.

It turns out I am trapped here, detained under section 5(2) of The Mental Health Act because I refused to consent to informal admission (of course, I did; I'm not mad). I'm vulnerable, risky, and in need of assessment.

'Seventy-two hours, Pippa,' Dr Kershaw answers my *how long* enquiry. 'Up to seventy-two hours, but you are being assessed for further detention under section 2, or 3. The police are yet to decide what route they will take, and it's unclear if you've been treated by mental health services before. Can you remember, Pippa, now that you're a bit more *lucid*?'

'Lucid?' Dr Kershaw really needs to work on his people skills. I heard seventy-two hours and zoned out trying to reckon if I'll be free in time for work on Monday. 'I can't, I'm afraid. I'm due back at work on Monday morning... You've been very kind, especially with the non-menopause diagnosis, but I really must be getting home. My (don't say Sadie; do not say Sadie). My boyfriend will be worried about me; we were supposed to be having a hot chocolate and...'

'Ben knows that you're here,' Diana interrupts. 'He's down as your next of kin...'

'Shhh,' I bat Diana away. Ben knows I'm here? Why has he not rescued me? Where *is* my car? Did Sadie get away from the flat? Did Dr Kershaw say something about me being a risk to others? Did he mean Heather and Cassandra? Keep calm, Pippa. Keep your Jacquetta on... 'I need a drink; where's the bar?'

'I'll get you some water in a second, Pippa. Ben, your sister... Heather and your mother will visit you later today. You might want to phone them and ask them to bring you some clothes and toiletries. Nothing sharp and no alcohol is allowed on the unit.' Diana sounds as though she has made this little speech countless times. I've already explained I'm allergic to alcohol. Perhaps I should meet the psychologist person; Diana and Dr Kershaw are far too dismissive of my questions. I wonder if Diana meant Sadie will be visiting later. I need to set her straight.

'Sadie is not my sister; she's my half-sister's half-sister.'

'Heather is your sister, Pippa, and like Ben, she's very concerned about you.' Diana and I have so much in common; neither of us likes to have our time wasted. Her words eventually sink into my brain (these drugs are potent). Heather is not dead; I am free to go. I don't care what this five two thingy is; I shall leave.

'So, Heather's not dead?' Shit! I immediately regret my words. 'I mean, no one was hurt...' I feign amnesia. 'You said I was found in the middle of a roundabout, was there any damage?'

Both Dr Kershaw and Diana battle to answer my many questions. 'Heather is alive and well, as far as I know, Pippa,' Dr Kershaw is disinterested as to why I asked (phew).

'The highways agency has not been in touch regarding your question about the central reservation. I have known things to drag on, in my experience, although it is not common for drivers to be admitted here.' Diana almost breaks confidentiality; what business is it of mine if my fellow inmates prefer public transport?

'And the man whose car you collided with was discharged from accident and emergency yesterday.' Patient confidentiality is flying all over the place, Dr Kershaw. I do not remember having a crash. I did not put a man in hospital.

'It wasn't me. None of this is my fault. Is it hot in here?' It is stifling in this room, and Diana has not fulfilled her promise of water *in a second*.

'You told the police that you would accept full responsibility,' Dr Kershaw lies; I did not speak to the police yesterday.

'Excuse me a moment while I fetch you some water, Pippa.' Diana mouths, *will you be alright?* to Dr Kershaw. I should drag Dr Kershaw to the exit by his lanyard and force him to open the door, but

I must tread carefully (especially as a huge mistake has been made).

'Could I have my phone call now, please?'

'You can make as many phone calls as you like, Pippa. Diana will show you to the patient phone when she returns with your water.' As Dr Kershaw speaks, I have a blurry recollection that my mobile was confiscated last night.

Chapter Twenty-Six

'Police, please,' I whisper into the telephone handset. Diana directed me to the patient phones and was good enough to explain how to give the handset a wipe down before and after use. Although I am allowed to use the patient phone, I must not take liberties. Fear not, Diana, this call will cost the NHS nothing; I'm contacting the emergency services.

'Are you in immediate danger?' I am asked, to which I reply that I am. I am so annoyed at Dr Kershaw, or whichever one of his friends gave me the tongue swelling medication. The difficult conversation I have with the call operator does not last much longer; they have my location. It is established that I am a patient asking to be rescued from The Mary Shelley Unit. I am under the care of mental health services, and therefore unlikely to require intervention from the police (especially not to release me from Dr Kershaw's orders or arrest NHS staff for pilfering). Before I start thinking this is a massive campaign against me, I remember this is all a misunderstanding. Then I recall Dr Kershaw's report of my car crash. If this is true, it wasn't my fault (and I probably shouldn't be talking to the police). Sadie sent me out there like a dozy hit man, slaying siblings in my pyjamas.

I think about who I shall phone next, but I

haven't memorised Ben's mobile phone number. I glance at Diana picking her nails a few metres away from the patient phone area. Keeping my cool, I plan to nonchalantly ask if I may obtain Ben's phone number from my mobile. Killing two birds, I shall know if the ward staff *did* steal my phone and connect the relevant line to my rescuers. Holding the phone's handset in my right hand, I approach Diana. Just as I got her attention, the sirens start wailing again, and Diana faces a dilemma. Should she escort me away from the area to ensure the phone handset is Covid free or should she respond to the alarm? I sense that these nurses are overworked and overstretched. I must get in Diana's good books.

'Could you stay here for me, Pippa?' Diana has made a decision.

'Of course, it would be my pleas...' I attempt cheery, but Diana is gone.

'Did you phone the police?' It is Mr Nosy, and he has read my mind. 'That's why they take our mobiles off us so that we can't ring the emergency services. Don't worry though, the smoke alarms are connected to the Fire Service. Don't bother trying to set one of them off though, that's where she's gone,' Mr Nosy nods towards the fleeing Diana. I wonder what his real name is.

'I'm Andy, and I've been in and out of this lockup ever since it was built. It's all a mistake, though; I've been fitted up.'

'I'm Pippa,' I offer a handshake but quickly withdraw it because of Covid; (I am trying to get in Diana's good books). Andy is also here under false pretences; we shall be friends.

'You keep watch, I'm just going to make a quick phone call,' Andy picks up the handset like a naughty schoolboy. I offer him an antibacterial wipe. 'You don't believe in all that Covid shit, do you? It's all conspiracies... hang on; it's ringing. Hello!' Andy has a loud telephone voice. 'Can I speak to Gary Neville? Yes, he does love; I've seen him on the telly. I just want to tell him I DON'T accept his apology.'

He must have had a ding dong with his friend Gary, who works in television.

'Get me Gary Neville, NOW, love. I don't like it when people waste my time!'

Andy and I have so much in common.

His phone call did not last long either. He slammed the phone down. He slammed it, then picked the handset up again and started hitting the wall-mounted dial pad with it. I was so shocked that I didn't hear Diana and her friends running towards him I had failed to keep watch. A siren alerted them to Mr Nosy's tantrum, and they came to tidy him up. This is what he must have meant by *always get a witness.*

'Are you alright, Pippa?' Diana approached me after Andy was taken away. I don't answer at first. If disagreeing with a football pundit has suddenly become an indicator of insanity, then goodness knows what could incriminate me. 'How's your tongue doing? It should have gone down by now.'

'I suppose I have recovered; it just feels a bit weird,' I answer because the tongue thing is the fault of this place. I expect my new friend has been sedated from the same batch after his outburst. Does being angry make you mad? I'm not cross at all; I was just following Sadie's orders yesterday. Penance for my guilt.

'I'll come back and have a walk round the courtyard with you if you like. I just need to... sort something out, Pippa. I'll be back in a second.'

I could be here a while, so I started to collect the breakages. I sense another pair of eyes is on me at a different square pane of glass. I vaguely recognise him; I hope what Dr Kershaw said isn't true. I haven't been here before.

'Hello, are you our new cleaning staff? Where's your PPE?' It is Mr Sparks (what are the fucking chances?).

'No, I do not work here. Someone had an accident with the payphone,' I gesture towards the remnants of Andy's smashing time. Recognition creeps across Mr Sparks' face.

'Pippa, come away from there, love. You might hurt yourself on those broken bits,' Diana returns to the scene of Gary Neville's rebuttal, cutting the atmosphere between Mr Sparks and me. 'This is Lee Sparks, Pippa; he's our ward manager. You know I told you about having a word with him after his meeting.'

'Pippa joined us last night, Lee. She wants to talk about going home.' I hear Diana whisper two words to Mr Sparks *she's sectioned.*

'I wouldn't mind that stroll round the garden you promised, Diana.' As I speak, I note a flicker of amusement between Mr Sparks and Diana. 'Chop-chop; I could do with a bit of fresh air.' I will not acknowledge Mr Sparks' previous meeting with me; Jacquetta would always keep the upper hand in a scenario such as this. Always.

Diana opens the door to the courtyard without any key-jangling or fuss. The way out from this place is managed by a series of magnets that dangle from Diana's neck. They've made a blunder here, especially as those lanyards are probably the quick release kind. Although, I remember the speed with which Diana answered that siren. She may well receive a starring role in any enquiry as to why Andy was allowed to use the patient phone unsupervised. I don't want to ruin her day any further.

The courtyard is a small enclosed outdoor space in the corner of a bigger garden. There is evidence that ashtrays have recently been removed; thank goodness I have no vices. I breathe the crisp outside air as though I have been deprived of it for much longer.

'Did you manage to get through to your boyfriend on the phone?' Diana asks.

'No, I was going to ask if I may have a quick glance at my mobile to write his number down,' I smile.

'Oh,' Diana almost swears. 'Sorry, I had to leave you by the phone, didn't I? It's been hectic today. Bear with me, and we can sort that out when we go back inside. You need to speak to Lee as well, don't you?'

I don't answer, because over Diana's shoulder I notice a large tree with dark fruits in the bigger garden.

'Is that a mulberry bush?' I ask.

'What? That thing? It's a tree; it's always been there, Pippa. I think they built the unit around it; there are no berries on it, though. It wouldn't do to be in a place...' Diana pauses to choose her words. 'It wouldn't be appropriate to have a tree that grows berries in a hospital.'

'Can I see it?'

'Not right now,' Diana senses the urgency in my voice. 'You have a chat with Lee about your stay here.'

'I just want to have a closer look, Diana. I swear I can see red fruits hanging on it,' I am not seeing things.

'Better not to discuss it out here, but you might be able to... I have known patients who were discharged home straight from here without being transferred,' Diana says.

'Transferred?'

'Yes, transferred to the wards that can access

that part of the garden,' Diana smiles and guides me back inside. I can't even go around the mulberry bush yet.

Chapter Twenty-Seven

'**I**f you like, Pippa, I could have one of my colleagues step in and manage your care.' Mr Sparks has a gentle tone about him, but I have no idea what he means. 'Because we are virtually neighbours, you may not want me to be part of your stay here as we live on the same estate.'

'The Peacock isn't part of the estate.' Mr Sparks is wrong about many things, ownership of India Kitten, and that Mummy's pub is included in the concrete jungle. Still, better the devil you know is an incantation I have grown to trust over the years.

'It would be no trouble, but I would still be the ward manager. If you decide to not make any changes to your care team, I assure you that you will be treated with the same professional courtesy that I practise with everyone. Your information and any conversations we have will be treated in the strictest confidence; unless you tell me that you've murdered someone.' Mr Sparks is deadly serious. 'You can trust me, Pippa.'

'That's where you're wrong, Mr Sparks. I can't trust anyone.' Am I opening up to the catnapper? It must be his approach.

'Do you think that might be part of the problem?'

I don't answer.

'We can get to that, but first, we need to discuss your request to go home, don't we?'

'Yes, please,' I cross my legs.

'The thing is, and I know it has been explained to you, you are detained under section 5(2) of the Mental Health Act.'

'This is getting boring, Mr Sparks. I was mistakenly deemed a threat to society last night, but now look at me; I'm a picture of innocence.' This is ridiculous.

'I'm sorry you're bored, but the thing is, the admitting doctor, the police, and your family were very worried about you yesterday. When you arrived here, you made demands for the night nurse to release you. You wanted to speak to someone called Sadie,' Mr Sparks continues with his gentle tone.

'Making demands? What's wrong with that?' I cannot believe how wretched this is.

'It's a nice way of saying you *kicked off.*' Mr Sparks' eyes beg forgiveness. 'You needed to get out so that you could ask Sadie if she still wanted you to kill Cassandra.'

'Hmm,' must be careful what I say here. 'Yes, your night nurse took my mobile phone away, so how else was I supposed to speak with her?'

'But, you wanted to talk to her about murder, Pippa.'

Shit.

'And the night nurse suspected that this Sadie person is a figment of your imagination.'

'Well, she's wrong,' I am angry now.

'You must understand that all these people, these healthcare *professionals,* are worried about you. You must see why they assessed you as a risk to others... and to yourself.' Mr Sparks needs to work on his open-ended questions.

'I have no intention of killing myself, Mr Sparks. Even though I have had a recent disappointment in my pet-owning life, I have a lot to live for. My boyfriend is about to take over The Peacock, I've recently reconnected with my half-sister's half-sister, and I have a good job doing sums... I mean accountancy,' I am out of breath. I'd better calm down before Mr Sparks calls in the cavalry. 'Sorry, it's just I'm a little concerned that Mr Bland will be upset with me if I don't arrive for work on Monday morning.'

'Is Mr Bland your boss?' Mr Sparks asks calmly.

'Yes, he's a wonderful boss, and I work with a wonderful receptionist.' Calm the fuck down, Pippa.

'Is he bland?' Mr Sparks smiles at me, and I smile back.

'No! That really is his name; I think he told me it's his family or something, from Yorkshire somewhere.' Am I being warmed up?

'He's lucky; everyone thinks I'm an electrician,' Mr Sparks laughs at his own joke, and I laugh too. 'I'm glad you've got all these positive things going on in your life, Pippa. And I'm sorry about the kitten, we can get onto that; perhaps you could talk about how that made you feel with the psychologist. I know you've been referred. Dr Schofield is very good at his job.'

'Dr Schofield?'

'The psychologist, like the nursing staff – me included, you can use his first name if you prefer, but I'll let you decide that with him.' Mr Sparks' discussion with me ends here, and he continues with a speech.

I asked no further questions but listened to Mr Sparks explain that my Covid test was negative, and that I am currently held in the intensive care unit of The Mary Shelley Unit. This is the only mixed ward in the mental hospital and is virtually impossible to get out of. Mr Sparks corrects himself here and inserts the word 'escape'. Still, I needn't worry. I will get out eventually when I'm transferred to the female ward and then discharged. I cannot appeal against my section to the mental health tribunal or hospital managers until it is converted to section 2 or 3. Dr Kershaw will need to speak with me again about my medication when my blood results are back. This is very boring, and I have already decided against forcing Diana to open the doors when Mr Sparks concludes his monologue. The poor lamb has enough on her plate.

'There's obviously something going on, Pippa and as strange as it seems, we are here to help you.'

'Nothing is going on, and I don't need help. You are welcome to dole out my share to someone needier than I.'

'I'm about to tell you the most important bit, Pippa.'

'And you have my full attention, Mr Sparks.' He has already requested that I call him 'Lee' several times, and his patience is wearing thin.

'Your family tell us that you have not been speaking to anyone called Sadie.'

'I have, Lee; they just haven't *seen* her,' I give Mr Sparks my best Jacquetta.

'And that's what made the admitting doctor decide that you need help because talking to someone that no one else can see is usually a sign of hearing voices.'

'That's what I mean, the doctor made a mistake; *I've* seen Sadie, but my family haven't!' Goodness, what a pickle. I know I sometimes fail to make myself understood, but... shit, I remember that Ben saw Sadie that first night.

'I think we're at crossed purposes here, Pippa. We can't legally let you go home tonight, but your case will be discussed in tomorrow's ward round. The consultant is very thorough.'

'There are no crossed wires at my end Mr Sparks!' There was only so long I could keep my cool. I'm being held here against my will by a child and a catnapper. Mr Sparks' speech is ended by my rant. I couldn't say exactly what I was shouting about... something along the lines of disgust that the nursing staff broke confidentiality by speaking with my family. Fun fact; families *can* spin nurses a tale, and nurses are allowed to listen. They just can't answer without the patient's consent. Heather, Jacquetta, and even Ben have framed me like a wailing banshee (minus the baby).

Just because you're paranoid doesn't mean they're not whispering about you.

Chapter Twenty-Eight

'Pippa, I needed to speak to you about your medication. But right now, the nursing staff feel you would benefit from a PRN – that means given when necessary – dose of one of the benzodiazepines; that means tranquiliser. Will you accept it?' Although speaking to me as he would a numpty, Dr Kershaw at least asks me this time.

'Don't give me any more of that tongue swelling stuff,' I am annoyed; anyone would think they are goading me on purpose.

'No, of course, Pippa; you were given emergency drugs last night because of how upset you were.'

I hold out my hand to accept the cleaner offering, I don't want to, but I sense that every conversation I enter will rub me up the wrong way. It wasn't me that was upset; it was the night nurse. Telling tales on her will only end in sirens and accusations of hysteria.

'Hold on, Pippa, I need to discuss something with you. Remember when I asked you about how much you've been drinking?' Dr Kershaw has me seated and sedated.

'Diana gave me some water earlier,' I say.

'I meant before your admission to this hospital, I need to know how much alcohol you were drinking.'

'I told you, I don't drink. I'm allergic to it, in the sense that it doesn't agree with me.'

'It's just that I wasn't sure about your account, so I sent your blood sample for an urgent LFT screen. It's important, Pippa, that we know how much you've been drinking because you may go into withdrawals, and that can be very dangerous.'

'Well...' I open my mouth to speak, the tickling sensation has returned to my throat, and I'm glad of it this time.

'Pippa, the truth is your blood results indicate you have been drinking heavily.'

'They've made a mistake.'

'The blood result confirmed your presentation.'

'I haven't given a presentation!'

'I meant I could tell by looking at your physical indicators... such as stomach problems and other things. Your whole presentation pointed to heavy drinking, and the blood results confirm it. Pippa, I need to put you on an alcohol withdrawal regime. It's similar to the drug I just gave you, plus vitamins to replace those not absorbed by someone who drinks heavily.'

'Very well... I shall comply. Get it over with, Dr Kershaw,' I get ready to accept yet more pills. If I ever make it to work on Monday, I shall be rattling.

'Pippa, an alcohol detox regime lasts for ten days.'

The shame I feel right now is horrendous, and

I just can't get my head around it. It is increasingly likely that Ben will not be able to rescue me, which means I shall have to admit to Mr Bland that I am a raging alcoholic. Dr Kershaw thinks I am avoiding telling the truth, but the fact is I have no answers for him about my alcohol use because I haven't even confessed it to myself yet.

Medicated again, I am escorted to my room and advised to lie down while Diana keeps her eyes on me from just outside the door. As I closed my eyes, I noted that Diana had full access to her own mobile... I forgot to phone Ben.

I'm not sure how long I lay there staring at the ceiling, but Diana has been replaced by one of her friends. This colleague introduces herself as Jane, and she tells me that I was asleep for a little while. I drink some water, and my diagnosis comes flooding back to me. Dr Kershaw's detective work has paid off, and I have been exposed as nothing but a common drunk. I thought my cloak was a success; it wasn't...

'Did you hear the news about me?' I ask Jane.

'What news?' Jane automatically reaches for her mobile phone, but then thinks better of it.

'They've found out what's wrong with me, Jane. I'm an alcoholic,' I practise saying it out loud. Soon, I will have to take responsibility (whether I want to or not).

'Well,' Jane enters my room and closes the door behind her. 'There's probably more to it than that, Pippa.'

'No, there isn't; Dr Kershaw said I have to do a detox,' my legs dangle off the side of the bed.

'It might be that you were drinking as a way of dealing with something. It's perfectly natural to look for a way of coping, especially with everything going on in the world. We just need to help you find a way of handling what life throws at you without putting your health at risk.' Jane is well practised with her promises.

I am sobbing, sobbing like someone who needs a drink. Jane has a point.

'It's alright, Pippa, you have a good cry. You might feel better for it, especially as you've been through so much in the last couple of days. Once you've had a glass of water or cup of tea, would you like to come to the relaxation session in the day room before visiting time?'

'What is it?' I wipe my nose on my sleeve, and Jane passes me a tissue and then nods at my discarded face mask.

'I'll get you a fresh one of those so that you can join in. Relaxation is good for everyone; it's like breathing and meditation. You've heard of mindfulness?'

'Hippy shit? Free on the NHS?' I accept Jane's face mask, and she smiles at my repartee.

'Yes, Pippa, free on the NHS.'

The day room has been modified (I presume within NHS standards) to resemble the women's retreat with more space and less whimsy. Minus the candles, minus hormone imbalance, minus the smell of incense, this space of dim lighting will help me see clearly.

Apart from Andy, this is the first time I have met my counterparts. I try to control my face, but I eye them with suspicion. Mr Sparks told me this is an eight bedded ward, yet only four people lie on the relaxation mats, five including me.

'Don't worry, Pippa. No one is going to force you to do anything you don't want to do. Give the session a try, and if it's not for you, you won't have to do it again.' Jane settles down onto one of the mats. Is she joining in? I suppose she deserves a perk of the job. 'I'll be right here next to you, making sure you're alright.' The settling rigmarole feels fuss-free today, and I am quite happy to stay.

The person providing this session is an occupational therapist named Iona. I started thinking about how I always thought Iona was a boy's name; today's Iona is female. This triggers a thought process about my own name, Epiphany. Then I start thinking about Mummy. Mummy and Heather...

Heather and Cassandra sitting in a tree, dead as a dodo when I am freed.

I've even written a poem; I hope I remember it when I get out of here. I start to imagine Heather and Cassandra sitting in that mulberry bush on the hospital grounds. It's not a bush; it's a tree. Diana's words echo around my mind on a warm and convivial Sunday.

'It is perfectly natural for your mind to start wandering during this session, but try to remember that you are here to focus on now. Now we are lying on the comfortable relaxation mats. Now we have this time to focus on ourselves.' Iona must have read my mind. She speaks with a voice that sounds as good as hot chocolate on a hygge day. Anymore of this, and I shall be imitating Iona. Oh, how I long for a beautiful voice. Do these thoughts count as focusing on me? Who is Epiphany? Epiphany the alcoholic? Pippa, the liar? I'm not lying now; I'm just lying down having a rest, turning my mind off.

Finally, in this weird scenario of dimmed lighting and enforced relaxation, I have the chance to recover. No one is forcing me to do anything except for me. Here is an opportunity to redeem myself.

'Now is your chance to recover because everyone deserves the chance to recover.' Iona continues with her telepathy.

I like Iona. I like the thingy I'm involved with now. I can do it, I can breathe, I am floating, I will not sink, and I can have more practice. I don't need drink; I don't need Sadie.

'Are you alright, Pippa?' Jane interrupts my

calm but only because she has cause for concern. I sat bolt upright, but now I can't move. I'm thinking about *The Miller's Tale*, the flood-fearing miller and his wench. She is long as a mast and upright as a bolt. *The Pardoner's Tale* is a story that can only be told by a drinker. I've got to confess, I'm in a real mess. I lied to my lover; I lied to my mother. My sister drove me to drink. I try not to think. I sit here, ready to face my demons. If I sink, I recover without Sadie. If I float, I return to a life of frumpy, fair, and almost forty. I think I prefer my chances on the ducking stool.

'If you're having trouble controlling obstructive thoughts, recognise they are simply thoughts and like breathing; this is what minds do. Your mind thinks, and your body breathes,' Iona directs her words for me without naming me. I like her, and I appreciate whatever this is.

The session comes to an end, and I have just lived my best forty minutes. I waited forty years for an epiphany, and three come along all at once. I didn't kill India, I realised my mother and sister are witches, and Iona has given me the revelation that thoughts are merely thoughts; they can't hurt me.

Iona wraps up the session, and although I would ordinarily be glad that it didn't last as long as some events, I am conscious that I cannot move. The same thing is happening again...

I am rooted to the spot. Andy has plenty to say about my rigidity, but I know that Dr Kershaw and Diana were careful not to repeat the dyskinetic overdose. Jane is duty-bound not to explain to Andy what is happening to me, and he is escorted away. Poor lamb, I shall explain all once I am freed from my body's trap. For now, I cannot even smile (which should come in handy because I sense that visitors are on the way).

Chapter Twenty-Nine

Visiting time did not last long and was split into two parts, for me anyway.

My friend Andy had just the one visitor, his wife, I presume. She wore spectacles, a bobble hat (indoors) and had a very severe fringe. And she did not smile back when I attempted to smile at her. My eyes are no longer the window to my soul; I am rooted to the spot. Andy playfully rolls his own eyes – he understands what is going on because he's already been here. The couple slopes off to a private location, and apart from milling nursing staff, I am alone again in the dayroom.

'Pippa!' It is Ben, and he appears to have lost a bit of weight; he has the cheekbones of a man who missed his last meal. I read envy and admiration all around me. I cannot answer Ben verbally or otherwise. 'I was so worried about you when you just drove off. I didn't know what to do. I even went to the nature reserve to see if you had forgotten I was going with you for a hot chocolate.'

Ben's fingers caress my hands, and it all floods back to me. I wonder if Sadie was still in our bedroom when Ben allowed me to escape.

'I'm sorry; it was just that you didn't come back.'

I wonder what Ben is apologising for.

'And the way you'd been talking – you must know you weren't your usual self... I was scared that you might crash your car. I'm sorry, Pippa, it was me that phoned the police.' Ben put his face in his hands. Careful, Ben, they might incarcerate you for melancholy. Still, I suppose he did the right thing; I *did* crash my car. I *was* my usual self, however – doing the bidding of a sibling is common practice in the life of Epiphany.

Seemingly, Ben tried to get the ward staff to snitch on me. Jane stepped in to facilitate a three-way conversation. Her attempt to gain my consent to discuss my care with Ben fell flat on its face. At least she had the decency to close the door to the room. Ben tries his *one blink for no* routine. As my eyelids start fluttering uncontrollably, Jane spills the tea about my problems. News travels fast, and Ben is unsurprised to hear that I have been drinking heavily because Jacquetta and Heather already betrayed me to him. Ben confirms that I definitely haven't been talking about murder, but I have been swearing more than I usually do during the past few days. Fortunately, Jane cannot remember the names I shouted to the night nurse (Heather and Cassandra). I keep quiet.

If only I could talk, I would ask Jane if nurses are rewarded for solving the riddle of confusion. I just sit and listen to Ben's report.

It all started when Ben spent a couple of

nights away from home. He does not allow Jane to question why he was away (most likely because this includes more accidental drinking). Ben remembers seeing me alone in a pub garden when he went out with Cassandra. There was a tiresome bit about Cassandra's lack of Tristan, which Jane did not need to know. All I could do was to listen. Apart from suspicion, the only other thing that Ben noticed was that I had started talking about someone called Sadie. Jane asks if Ben ever met this person, to which he lied and says no. I notice that my fingers don't respond to Ben's caress. I hope I remember to mention this once I am free from my trap.

Ben explains that I was just like this (mannequin version of Pippa) after returning home from a day out with my sister. Jane asks if I was given drugs. I was (for the crippling stomach pain); I try to shout 'cramps' as I had previously, but nothing comes out of my mouth.

Jane has some news. The man whose car I clipped does not intend to press charges (once he found out where I am). The police and DVLA may have another view, and I am apparently obliged to report my admission here. Jane tells me that in her *experience,* I won't be allowed to drive for at least three months after I'm discharged. They'll review it... Ben adds that I won't need my car because I can give up my job when we take over The Peacock (I shall be trapped without the jalopy). Jane opens her mouth, and I read she wishes to debate if owning and working in a pub is a good idea. She thinks better of it because she notices Mummy chomping at the bit to see me. Heather is flirting with Mr Sparks behind the reinforced glass.

'What are the CHANCES that Mr Sparks should be working here, Epiphany!' Heather pushes into the dayroom wearing one of the hospital masks. Mummy follows her with the same disguise; this must be awful for the pair of them. No doubt, my eternal gratitude will be expected for their conformity. 'He's the *ward manager*, Pippa,' Heather speaks to me as though I am hard of hearing.

'We won't have to send you to a private facility now that we know the running of this place is up to scratch,' Mummy adds. I am astounded to hear Jacquetta siding with the cat thief.

Jane opens her mouth again, but Heather has more to say. 'Come on, Ben, it's our turn to visit our little Pipsqueak. You've had your half an hour.'

'Don't worry me like that again, Pippa.' Ben throws his arms around me in farewell.

Jane ushers him out of the area, but Ben manages to ask Heather to write down his phone number. We can communicate in the old-fashioned way now that he has figured out the phone rule.

Alone at last with Heather, although I'm not alone, am I? Mummy and Jane are in the room, and in any case, I can't speak. No matter, I am unlikely to forget all the things I want to say to Mummy and Heather. And my questions will no doubt be answered within the words that Heather and Mummy wish to say to me. That covers my *immediate* questions; Heather and Mummy are unlikely to mention the coven before a registered mental health nurse. Magical thinking is probably one of the first things Jane learnt about during her training; the delusional connotations of sorcery. Am I the third member?

I drifted off then; it must have been my self-preservation habit.

'Pippa,' Heather clicks her fingers in front of my face.

'You don't mind if I say... I'm not sure that will help, sorry.' Jane apologises to Heather for Heather's own wrongdoing.

'Well, what on earth's the matter with her?' Heather points at me. We have to repeat the consent to share information rigmarole. I curse my eyelids for responding. If they moved a bit slower, then visiting time would be over, and I wouldn't have to listen to Heather disrespecting Florence Nightingale and all her friends.

'Look at her eyes for goodness sakes!' I cannot tell by Mummy's tone if she is berating Jane or me. Either one of us is at fault for my eye-rolling, but it is Jane who starts talking.

'Initially, the doctor thought this could have been side effects from the medication Pippa was given on admission,' Jane is a trooper. She survived the pandemic, now she must tackle the two most anti-psychiatry busybodies to ever grace visiting time at The Mary Shelley Unit. Even double-time would not be payment enough. Jane, I'd salute you (if I could).

'Side effects? Side effects? Side EFFECTS?' Heather repeated these two words with varying degrees of interrogation.

'All medication has side effects, and Pippa has had a thorough medication review since.'

'Well, it would be *helpful* if you could forward a list of any possible complications to the relatives BEFORE visiting time. Then there will be no nasty shocks.' Heather's sense of entitlement is mighty today.

'And we could have prepared a tincture of clove, ginger, and turmeric,' Mummy brings her unfiltered self to the table.

'Patients are not permitted to bring their own medication onto the unit, I'm afraid. Even herbal ones,' Jane stokes Heather's fire.

'Well, that's nonsense. What are you treating her for?' Heather speaks about me as though I am not here, but I don't mind because Jane glances at me, and I manage to twitch the non-verbal for *let her have it.*

'Pippa was brought here by the police after she crashed her car into a roundabout near Pendle. At the moment, Pippa is being treated with an alcohol detoxification programme. It is ward round tomorrow; Pippa will be assessed by Dr Carnegie, the consultant psychiatrist and Dr Schofield, the clinical psychologist. They don't think Pippa's presentation is due to side effects. More likely, this is extreme agitation,' Jane gently gestures in my direction.

Stick that in your pipe and smoke it, Heather.

'Near Pendle, sweetie,' Heather changes her tune. She is all things to all people.

'I think she'd had a bit of a tiff with lover boy. He called at my house locked out in his undergarments.' Mummy adds.

'Oh, and you drove straight to your older sister for a bit of love and guidance,' Heather gushes.

'And Ben drove you to drink, but you're safe now.' Is Mummy drunk?

'Well, she's always been safe, *Jacquetta*. Ben is about to unburden you from The Peacock after all these years.' Heather condescends that I am safe, if only in the hands of an enabler.

'Oh yes, that's right, we just need to make sure the other problem stays silent,' Mummy whispers in the same way she did when avoiding the word 'prison' when workmen were within earshot. She obviously means Cassandra, and Heather nods in return. I am so confused... If Heather thinks Cassandra is a usurper that puts Sadie at risk (even though she is my half-sister's half-sister).

Is it hot in here? Jane has said nothing of my suspected hallucinations. Does that mean she doesn't think I hear voices? Does Jane's assessment of me differ from Dr Kershaw's? I was hoping for a second opinion... Then Jane does the dirty on me.

'I must explain that I don't usually work on this ward, I'm just covering, so I only know what the previous nurse handed over to me. You know what it's been like with all of the pandemic problems,' Jane offers her way out; the reason she has not examined my case thoroughly is because of Covid. Heather and Mummy look at her blankly. 'I do know that Pippa was worried about her job earlier. Obviously, this passive state means that Pippa may not be able to speak with her boss.'

'I know Mr Bland very well, dear. I shall contact him first thing and explain that Pippa is drying out.'

'I wouldn't... Pippa's boss needn't know the details. Just explain that Pippa is in hospital because she's not well.' Jane is a pillar of trustworthiness.

'Mr Bland knows, young woman. Yes, he knows all about Pippa's drinking. We all did,' Mummy gives Jane her best Jacquetta.

It *is* hot in here, and I cannot breathe because the tickling sensation returns. I panic that Iona will not return in time with her breathing exercises when Jane takes control. She is good at her job, especially as she realised I was having an asthma attack and whisked Heather and Mummy away. My visitors departed with threats to manipulate the psychiatrist and folly driven denial of my respiratory complaint.

'It's been a long day, Pippa,' Jane's tone has

altered to one of settling. I remain mute; I don't mind, I have nothing more to say. My counterpart inmates mill around the ward in silence; some are gearing up, others merely ignorant of the time of day. I catch Jane's face moments before she looks away and nod my response. 'Would you like to try your night medication? We need to see if you're able to swallow them.'

After a few attempts, I manage to accept my tablets. Jane flustered that she may have to call out the duty doctor for advice and alternatives, but I managed to swallow them along with a few gulps of water. I have nothing to lose now. I can be easily persuaded.

'Do your mum and auntie always pretend that you haven't got asthma?' Jane gives me a concerned face, which turns into a smile when she sees me laughing. 'Oh dear, she's your sister, isn't she? I thought Heather was your aunt because she called your mum Jacquetta,' Jane laughs too.

'No,' I manage. The ward lights are dimmed further at the end of this mindful and awful Sunday. I close my eyes again and imagine Jane writing in my medical notes *responded appropriately to humour* as a sign of my recovery.

Chapter Thirty

I woke again sometime around the witching hour. I knew because the dimmer switches have reached total darkness. My room is lit only by the distant mobile phone screens of the night watch. Which reminds me, Heather did not write Ben's phone number down. She did that on purpose... I hope Ben knows about my forthcoming appearance in tomorrow's ward round. I miss Ben.

'I know you do,' Sadie's legs dangle off the side of the chair arm (did she just read my mind?).

'Sadie? ... What did you say?' Thank goodness my power of speech has returned; I have never been so glad to see a sibling as I am now.

'I said hello you,' Sadie stands to plump my pillow. She is wearing the same uniform as Diana wore earlier and those favourite stretchy leggings (what a rebel).

'Oh my God, is this where you work, Sadie?' I can't remember if I ever asked Sadie where she works.

'I'm here, aren't I sister?' Sadie's hair is tied back in a long plait, and her cheekbones look glorious to the fullest degree.

'Is it alright for you to be on duty here? Mr Sparks said something about nurses not being allowed to...'

'Shhh,' Sadie puts her finger on my lips (with no regard for the restrictions). 'It's not like you're going to kick-off, is it?'

'No,' I murmur.

'That's the only reason nurses aren't allowed to work on the same ward as their relative. It's so we don't have to be involved if the siren goes off for our own sister.' It is cute that Sadie thinks she's related to me. 'Anyway... last time we spoke was when we decided to bump Heather and Cassandra off.' Sadie smiles as though she is reminiscing about some hilarious and exclusive incident (in which you had to be there).

'I'm sorry, Sadie. I got as far as the big roundabout on the way to Pendle. I was trying to run Heather over... the next thing I knew I woke up in here. They think I'm hearing voices commanding me to kill.'

'Trying to run Heather over? Your favourite weapon – I like it,' Sadie is one cunning plan away from steepling her fingers. She thinks nothing of the hallucination accusation.

'I'm sorry, Sadie,' I don't want to fail her.

'It's fine,' Sadie bats me away. 'I used the envelope that Cassandra wrote on, remember the one you gave me from Ben's birthday card. You didn't tell me that Cassandra will be a silent partner; I would have known that my hex had worked.'

'A hex? You didn't get rid of her, Sadie; Cassandra's a silent partner. She'll still get your share of

The Peacock.'

'I know, but I charmed her to keep away from you, Pippa... You're welcome.' Where has Sadie been all my life?

'Do you know what the consultant will say to me tomorrow?' I ask although I'm probably not allowed to know what Sadie has read in my medical notes (she is my half-sister's half-sister).

'Yes... Oh, you want me to tell you? He will ask you if you're scared of being uprooted.'

'What?'

'He will see your insistence on keeping The Peacock as an undeniable sign that you are scared of being uprooted from your life... the way it is; frumpy, fair, and almost forty,' Sadie knows my rhyme. Shit. 'Don't worry; your treatment won't be about moving out of The Peacock. No, it will be looking at helping you to be happy. Sorting out what is stopping you from being content. Probably yourself, Pippa, if you're scared of being uprooted. It's perfectly natural to feel this way after the pandemic.'

'Everyone's favourite excuse,' I agree.

'It's not an excuse, Pippa. Covid is real; you shouldn't listen to everything the green goddess says.' Sadie would say this; she is in tune with the medical model.

We catch up and spend the following hour talking about witchcraft as though we are picking out new nail varnish colours. Sadie reckons that

Heather and Mummy were *only protecting* me by not disclosing their superpowers.

'I can't believe you haven't brought Mum's *Book of Fantastic Facts* with you to read,' Sadie says.

'I've only had one visiting time, and they didn't think to bring me any books.'

'I'll see what I can manifest for you next time I'm here.' Sadie reaches into her breast pocket and pulls out a hand-rolled cigarette and a lighter.

'You can't smoke that in here, Sadie. The smoke alarms are connected to the fire station.'

'Who told you that?'

'Andy,' my eyes widen. This scenario is similar to the time when Sadie tried to persuade me to get drunk.

'You believed him?'

'Yes, I did, Sadie. I'm surprised at you, working here, thinking that all mental patients don't know what's going on.'

'Ever thought he might be a plant?' Sadie sparks up her joint with conspiratorial closeness.

'Sadie! Is that what I think it is?'

'Yes... And Andy *is* a plant. The hospital managers pay him to live here to try and trick you out of your paranoia. He'll tell you stories about the smoke alarms to reduce damage to hospital property. Is he still going on about Gary Neville?'

'Yes.'

'There you are then; he needs to come up with a more up to date delusion. That one is boring. He's definitely a plant.' We are both toking on Sadie's bifta. Heather has never offered me such an exciting herb.

'You've got to tell them, Pippa. Otherwise, they'll think you are drinking for the sake of it. You've got to tell them you've seen me.' Sadie blows out smoke.

It is here that I realise what is really going on.

'I bet this is what psychosis feels like, not really knowing what is going on.' Sadie has not lost her touch; she can still read my mind.

'Yes, not knowing what's happening and feeling frightened,' I add to Sadie's theory of psycho-analysis.

Sirens sounded throughout the night, but I was half asleep. Almost awake with no intrusions, the treatment must be working already.

My counterpart inmates do not greet me during the morning rigmarole. Medication and breakfast are doled out in silence by the nursing staff. Listening to their conversations, I gather that the smoke alarms were set off sometime during the night. Then I remember it is ward round day, the day where we must succumb to controlling oppression. I can understand why institutionalisation breeds paranoia, and I have only been here less than seventy-two hours.

I see little point in attending to my personal hygiene and costume. Let the consultant see my true colours, and then a fact-based assessment can be formulated. I decide against walking in there naked and keep the clothes I have worn for the past few days.

'We're ready for you now, Pippa,' Diana is back on duty. She appears unsurprised that I am in complete control of my reflexes. No doubt Diana received the night nurse newsletter this morning. Still, I am glad to see her as she escorts me into the dayroom. It has been transformed once again into a round table type set-up. Heather and Mummy sit together in one corner (they must have convinced the ward staff they are in a 'bubble'). Diana takes a seat a few metres away from Mr Sparks, and there are two new people I haven't seen before. A woman and a man, they could be a married couple but for the distance between them.

'Hello, Pippa. I'm Dr Carnegie, your consultant psychiatrist,' the woman says. This is very confusing; I thought Dr Kershaw was my doctor.

'And I'm Dr Schofield, the psychologist. Please join us,' Dr Schofield waves his hand towards the centre of the circle. I stride forwards and sit on the floor.

'Pippa, sit on this chair,' Diana jumps up to rectify my faux pas.

'No, let Pippa sit on the floor if she wants to,' Dr Carnegie says. Ward round already feels like a family squabble.

'Maybe we should all sit on the floor?' Dr Schofield adds.

'No, really, it was my mistake. Thank you,

Diana, for the chair.' I will not have the nurse belittled in this public-schooled circle.

'I usually like to start with a summary of what brought the person I'm treating to hospital. Would that be alright with you, Pippa?' Dr Carnegie starts us off.

'Yes,' I avoid making eye contact with Heather and Mummy; I must stay strong and not come out with any weird agitations. I am fully compos mentis and can prove it.

True to its name, here we go round the past seventy-two hours in this long and tedious meeting. I have not improved during that time, so Dr Carnegie recommends my length of stay is converted to a section 2. I am in luck; Mr Sparks is AMP trained (whatever that is), he can legally provide the second opinion, and I won't have to meet a social worker. I suppose I should be grateful to the catnapper; section 2 is all about admission for assessment. My social life is very poor; a social worker would be sure to assess me as a lost cause.

The best bit of ward round is reading Heather's mind. She is a bit bored and drifts off. Heather imagines an entertaining scene in which she is the centre of attention, rather than me. She is held captive here because she is the most successful and beautiful green goddess ever, and psychiatrists from around the globe flock to revel in her tenacity. A woman so sure of her abilities has never been chanced upon before. Heather's self-assurance inspires a new entry into the ICD-10 *The Heather Syndrome.*

Mummy has no time for her own thoughts but spins a tangent about private healthcare. 'Being from the landed gentry, I fully intended to have my youngest daughter housed in a private asylum.'

I read that Dr Carnegie is beyond offended, but Mummy does not pick up on this. Heather grabs the talking stick and explains that upon realising Mr Sparks is ward manager, they viewed The Mary Shelley Unit as an appropriate place for my bedlam.

'No one gives an actual shit what you two think.' I just can't control myself any longer.

'You see, Epiphany doesn't usually use language like that... it must be the riff-raff rubbing off on her.' Mummy talks about me as though I am not here, and she has never sounded so upper middle class.

'Pippa is an adult and responsible for her own care,' Dr Carnegie defends me.

'Have you thought about family therapy?' Mr Sparks adds from out of nowhere.

'Oh goody; then we can invite your husband, Rhys,' I aim my words at Heather but look directly at Mr Sparks.

'We need to cover the foremost issues,' Dr Carnegie asserts her authority. She gives an explanation about my alcohol flush, although, I will not succumb to the pushing and pulling that accompanies this regime. Dr Carnegie thinks I look a bit over sedated today; she threatens to bring in another expert from the pharmacy department. Mr Sparks adds that it has been tricky medicating me because I refused to talk about how much alcohol I have been drinking. Dr Schofield says he can understand entirely, and Heather demands to meet the pharmacist. She wants to know what the medication is made of.

'Crushed bones? Animal fats? Chemicals?' Heather quizzes with loaded affirmations.

'Pippa will be referred to the alcohol support team, as is any patient treated with a detox. They are a community-based provision but provide in-reach on the wards for early engagement.' Dr Carnegie attempts a reply.

'I've been enlightened with alcohol from an early age; Mummy has always been a drinker,' I interrupt my own meeting.

'She doesn't know what she's talking about.' Mummy talks about me.

'Yes, I do, Mummy; you didn't know how old I was until I was at secondary school because you were so pickled. I tried to get you to ask the authorities for my birth certificate, but you always said that if you ask a lot of people the same question, all you get is a lot of different answers.' I talk about Mummy and include her in the conversation (and she thinks I'm the mad one).

'I think this is where I can step in, Pippa. I can

be the *one* person you speak to. And together we can find out what the answers are,' Dr Schofield steps up.

'I think that's a splendid idea. You know, Pippa, many of my patients think that the work Dr Schofield does is magic,' Dr Carnegie smiles.

'Magic?' as I ask this, I read the same question in Mummy and Heather's thoughts.

'What Dr Carnegie means is that psychologists use strategies. I don't prescribe medication, but I do believe in a holistic approach. Complex solutions for complex needs,' Dr Schofield is slightly irked by his medical model friend.

'Complex needs?' Am I a freak of nature?

'Research has shown psychological interventions improve intensive engagement for dual diagnosis patients,' Dr Schofield nods at me.

'Ah yes,' Mummy makes a fool of herself by purporting to have read these scholarly claims.

'What is dual diagnosis?' Heather latches on to these two words as I did with 'magic'.

'It means that Pippa...' Mr Sparks attempts, but Dr Schofield continues.

'Dual diagnosis is the term used in modern psychiatry for people suffering from a mental illness and have been drinking heavily simultaneously,' Dr Schofield explains.

'Schizophrenia and substance misuse,' Dr Carnegie says.

I read *I knew it* in Heather's mind.

'In your case, Pippa, we won't know if you

have a significant mental illness until we do a thorough assessment.' Dr Schofield adds.

'Assess away everyone. I'm already late for work,' I tense my muscles and pretend to lie prostrate, pivoting on the back and seat of the chair. Diana is shitting herself; she is one entry in the incident book away from a suspension. She stands to assist me in adjusting my position; everyone watches her struggle with me.

'Yes, what is your assessment of Pippa's... trance?' Heather struggles to find the right word, as does Dr Carnegie.

'Some of what happened to Pippa could have been a reaction to the medication she was given in an emergency.'

'Oh, we've been through this,' Heather gives her best stroppy teenager.

'Though I now believe it to be caused by agitation. Some people... and I think this is what's happening to Pippa, can take on a stupor. Similar to a dissociative state; you've heard of catatonia?'

I start singing.

'Be quiet, Pippa. I'm finally getting to find out what's wrong with you.' Heather is vexed, and I manage to be quiet. Diana conceals a smirk; she is such a professional.

'Catatonia is very rare; it is an indicator of schizophrenia, but I don't think this is what this is, especially because of the rapid turnaround of symptoms. I would say that Pippa's 'trance', as you put it is a symptom of anxious-avoidant personality disorder,' Dr Carnegie speaks.

'Rubbish! There must be more to it than that; Pippa has always buried her head in the sand,' said Mummy.

'There is more to it, Mrs...' Dr Carnegie has forgotten Mummy's name. She turns to me, but for all to hear. 'Pippa, you have appeared paranoid during the time you've been here. Phoning the police and attempting to make your escape.'

'I haven't tried to escape. Tell them, Diana!' I expect a bit of sisterhood from the young nurse after I resisted grabbing her lanyard.

'Not on my watch, Pippa. But the night staff had to restrain you for two nights on the run.' For the first time in her career, Diana holds the power. She repeats the night nurse's lies, and no one will doubt her because she is a qualified nurse. My phone call to the police was not connected, and the Fire Service was a waste of time when they arrived.

'Your florid symptoms do seem to trouble you at night, Pippa.' Dr Carnegie asks me and tells me at the same time (most efficient). 'This is why I wanted to speak with Pippa's next of kin. Ben? Where is Ben?'

'We asked him to stay at home because of the restrictions,' said Mummy (what a time to start heeding government guidelines).

'But I believe Ben has evidence about the person Pippa appears preoccupied with. Sadie?'

I read a collective 'now we're getting to it' in everyone's minds (including mine).

'Sadie was here last night, Doctor; she works here!' These people need to observe the duty roster from the previous seventy-two hours. Sadie's name will be there, and my story will be confirmed, allowing me to go home.

'Staff Nurse Vickie was on duty last night,' Diana takes the Cathy from my Heathcliff.

'And so was Sadie,' I say.

'Sadie? India's daughter Sadie? Is that who you mean, Pippa? That's impossible!' Mummy and Heather are horrified.

'No, she *works here*, and she told me I had to tell everyone I've seen her – otherwise, you'll all think I'm a complete nut job.'

'Epiphany,' Mummy starts to tell me off. 'No one has seen Sadie for seven years; she ran off with your father. Sadie was Nancy to Maddox's Bill Sikes and all to prove a point to her mother. Their car was found abandoned near some cliffs in Pembrokeshire.' Mummy delivers her theory with a bristling mix of disgust and sorrow.

'What?' I don't believe this for one second; I can't believe it because this will make me look foolish. Sadie *was* there in my flat wearing sexy leggings listening to my woes with her long, dark hair. I didn't imagine her, and if Ben were here, he would set everyone straight. Ben saw her. Ben telephoned me at work with a message about my sister visiting.

'Sadie is probably... Sadie's been declared dead, Pippa. Recently... along with your father, you knew this Pippa,' Heather fills in the gaps.

'They went missing seven years and two months ago, come to think of it. Around the time of your episode...' Mummy is about to add fuel to the fire with another lie about my stability.

I read Dr Carnegie's mind; she has just figured out that Sadie is my half-sister's half-sister who had an affair with my father. What an interbred nest of vipers (she concludes).

Chapter Thirty-One

My mental state worsens over the next few weeks, and I drag the ward down with me. Even Jane's idioms show signs of apathy. 'Sometimes, Pippa, things have to get worse before they get better,' she tells me one Sunday afternoon. Poor lamb; I'd be depressed too if I had her job (treating people who don't think they need treating – or in my case, don't need treatment).

Ben has become big chums with Dr Carnegie, and they have regular chats about my home life. How I kept my drinking secret, so secret that even I didn't know about it. Ben confirms that Jacquetta is also a lush and Heather a herbalist. After a few days of not knowing where to turn, I decided to take Ben at face value. On the surface, Ben's insistence on 'taking care of me' is almost nauseating. He brings me books (the wrong ones, I have read all of these), and he brings me flowers (not allowed on hospital property). Ben is only doing his duty when speaking about me as though I'm not here. He's all I've got.

Shockingly, Mummy and Heather deny any and all traces of witchcraft. Who can blame them? They saw how quickly I was sectioned and re-sectioned like seasoned chicken drumsticks ready for the fryer. Mummy assures me that my job is safe and has shared the details of my neurotic collapse with Mr Bland and Karen. Heather continues to blow the whistle on my historical profile. Even though Mr Sparks defends my honour as a cat lover, Jacquetta spins a tale about the time I tried to drown the family cat. Beauty (the cat in question) did not mind my twelve-year-old experiment. I was not trying to drown her; I was simply trying to determine if cats sink or swim (I was subsequently assessed by a child psychologist). This is all hurriedly documented in my permanent record. Later that day, Mad Annie confirms that families are always believed before the patient. Always. She was known as 'Annie' until her ex-husband branded her a psychopath.

Sadie has not returned either for night duty or in my preoccupations. An Oxford Classics copy of *Selected Letters* by Charlotte Bronte appears on my bed one day. I presume this is a manifestation from Sadie but Andy spoils it for me. He will be transferred to the men's open ward later today, and the book was a goodbye gift to me. He promises to visit me via the railings inside the hospital grounds. It's a lovely book, but I just don't have it in me to read at the moment. I am neither driven nor hopeless; I am simply flat. As flat as a fucking pancake.

I am fully dried out now, and it is as though I have never drunk a drop. There is chatter at medication time about my habit being *not as bad as first thought.* Every day I take the vitamins and piss very expensive piss. I don't miss what I don't remember having, and I avoid any pushing and pulling concerning withdrawal symptoms and cravings for alcohol.

Another ward round comes and goes. This time, Ben manages to reserve a seat at the table. Dr Carnegie has a suspicion that my symptoms point to a complex delusional system – but I shouldn't worry; that is not as bad as it sounds. Because my misconceptions were grandiose, I am less likely to commit suicide. I read Diana's mind; she will be keeping a close eye on me when the psychoactive drugs start to work, and I realise I've made a massive fool of myself. At least I have that to look forward to.

Then Dr Carnegie says something, and everyone agrees apart from me. Her prescriptive write up almost sends me back to square one, making demands of the nursing staff (or kicking off, as I like to call it).

'I need to send you for a brain scan, Pippa. A CT scan,' Dr Carnegie says.

'No, thank you,' I repeat my original argument about spending public money elsewhere (and congratulate myself for keeping my cool).

'I want to check if there is any unusual activity going on in your brain, Pippa. It would be remiss of me and dangerous for you if I didn't.'

'I don't want you to read my brain; it's private.'

I ignore the humour that Mr Sparks and Diana see in my protest and curse myself for laughing with Sadie about Cassandra's unfortunate nostrils. Karma *is* a bitch.

'I'm not discounting your history, Pippa. I've read the notes made by the child psychologist after your feline torture episode and the suspected erotomania you suffered involving your friend's husband. Still, I want to rule out an organic cause for your behaviour.'

'Organic?' damn my green goddess sister.

'Pippa, I want to rule out anything like a tumour or a brain bleed. Disturbance around or pressuring the frontal lobes of your brain can affect thought processes.' Dr Carnegie speaks bluntly, and Ben looks as though he is about to collapse. If I sink, I have brain cancer, and if I swim, I am schizophrenic (what a catch).

'Either way, your symptoms can be treated with psychology,' Dr Schofield gives me hope. I must tell him about Sadie.

At recreation time (model's own words), I sit back to back in the garden with Andy with only the intensive care railings between us. I have swapped one addiction for another; Andy has taken me to his dealer. He rolls secret funny fags, and in return, I listen to his problems. Occasionally, we get caught. Andy's wife is currently annoyed at him because although he is on a male-only ward, she has a potential love rival on the women's side of the unit. Lucy hardly needs to be here; she already has an established coping strategy (albeit maladaptive) for her upsets. Andy sees this as a big problem, women are continually throwing themselves at him, and his wife is wretched of it. At least he is at no risk to himself.

'Sadie said you're a plant, Andy. Is that true?' I venture.

'Who the fuck is Sadie?' Andy defends.

'I thought she was my half-sister's half-sister, but the psychiatrist says I imagine her,' I exhale.

'So really, you imagined me to be a plant,' Andy takes the joint out of my fingers. 'Do you think I would be disregarding any of the current guidelines about Covid infection if I wasn't really a mental case?'

'An almost recovered one, I suppose. I'm sorry, I suspected you, Andy. You're a good friend.'

'I'll never recover, Pippa. But at least I have insight now,' Andy looks forlorn.

'Watch out, Andy, ten o'clock in the women's courtyard. I think your girlfriend has just come out to play.'

And with that, Andy was gone. I did suffer Lucy's dirty looks for the rest of the evening, but that's nothing. I grew up with Heather; Lucy wouldn't know what to do with an Epiphany, even if she had one.

Chapter Thirty-Two

Today is my first appointment with Dr Schofield, and I don't know what to wear.

This will be like an excursion from the ward. I shall be escorted to and from Dr Schofield's consulting room by Grace Poole. My obedience will be observed and documented in my medical notes for future assessment. I have been told (in several different ways by several different health professionals) that I am still considered a risk to others because I will not accept that Sadie is an illusion. I tried to tell Diana (she seemed the most gullible) that Sadie has changed her mind about bumping Heather and Cassandra off. She wouldn't have it but reassured me that changing *my* mind about murder is a sign of recovery. Diana doesn't know what she's talking about; I didn't want to kill anyone. It was all Sadie's idea.

I evaluate all the clothes that Ben has brought to the ward for me. I could wear Sadie's shiny leggings, but I am unable to without mentioning her. Quite frankly, I have had enough of talking about Sadie. After all, the whole idea of therapy is to talk about oneself.

No doubt, Dr Schofield will assess my every non-verbal murmur. I struggle to choose an outfit that portrays needy but not that crazy. Duplicity is a tiresome affliction, but in the end, I choose a khaki jumpsuit teamed with a fun bumblebee belt. A great idea (until I need to use the bathroom).

Body confidence out of the window, I am ready to have my mind read by a clinical psychologist.

'Hello, Pippa. You're a little late,' Dr Schofield welcomes me into his room, and my keeper indicates she will wait outside (a tedious job and a waste of NHS resources). I'm not late; it wasn't my fault I had to be escorted to the psychology corner of the building. Dr Schofield must have an obsessive streak, poor lamb. I walk into his consultation room which smells of antiseptic, eucalyptus, and unburdening. There is no sign of a couch, and I am guided to a chair next to but not directly opposite another chair belonging to Dr Schofield. 'Unless you want to sit on the floor?' he offers a cheeky grin.

'No, I'm fine here, thank you,' I've just realised Dr Schofield doesn't need an answer.

'So, Pippa... Or do you prefer Epiphany?'

'Pippa,' I give a hurried and forthright explanation about my name, and why I don't like it. Dr Schofield writes something down.

'Pleased to meet you, Pippa... I like both my names; you can either call me Dr Schofield or Luke.' The psychologist is proud of his labels. I expect he is making up for some childhood trauma.

'Did people used to call you Luke Skywalker at school?' I haven't decided yet how I shall address this person.

'Yes, they did,' Dr Schofield answers with a *'we're not here to talk about me'* tone.

'What is Dr Carnegie's first name?' Shit. Luke looks at me with accusations of transference. I'm not being deceptive; I just need all the facts.

'Erica,' Dr Schofield gives it a moment's thought, and then capitulates; I still haven't decided what I shall call him yet. 'How are you spending your time on the unit?'

This is a fairly innocuous question, but I must consider my answer. Is Dr Schofield making small talk, or is he referring to my night-time activities? I just can't settle during the graveyard shift, restless at the slightest noise because it might be Sadie. I asked the night nurses when Sadie will be back on duty, but this only resulted in sirens and sedation (to be fair, I did try to break into the nurses' station to have a look at the roster).

'It's ok, Pippa; I'm just making small talk. I'm asking what you've been doing to occupy your time.' Luke is a mind reader.

'I have started smoking.' I smile.

'Oh,' Luke says (I don't think smoking was what he had hoped for).

'And my boyfriend brought me some books to read... I just can't read them.'

Luke replies with a nod.

'I can't concentrate.'

'That's a common complaint, Pippa. Mental instability can disturb concentration and makes reading frustrating and unpleasant.'

'You're right! I usually love reading; I love books... all the books... usually.'

'I would recommend trying to continue. Read something pleasant and uplifting. Remember; you are reading for pleasure, reading to relax. No one will ask you for a synopsis, so it doesn't matter if you follow the story or not. If reading is something you enjoy, this is a good way to try and carry on with it. Practice makes perfect if you like.'

'Well, the thing is I do like to follow the story; otherwise, there's no point in reading it.'

'The *point* is, I'm advising that you read to relax,' Dr Schofield repeats his message.

'Like the breathing exercise thingy?'

'Exactly; now, just out of interest, what do you like to read?'

'Recently, I've been reading Agatha Christie. Someone told me that her books are the best cure for heartbreak – because they are nothing to do with romance.' I skate dangerously close to the Sadie disclosure here.

'Have you read The Pale Horse? It's quite different to Christie's other works... it's the one about witchcraft,' Luke offers himself as a thera-peutic tool, and I am terrified. I can't remember what I have said and what I haven't.

'I'm not heartbroken, though... it was all a misunderstanding.' I change the subject again.

'Ben, is your boyfriend's name?'

'Yes, I thought he... he stayed away from home

for two nights. Sorry, I don't want to talk about it; it's all forgotten now.'

'What would you like to talk about, Pippa? I'm ready to believe you.'

'Like on *Ghostbusters*?'

'Just like it. Do you *want* to talk about ghosts?' Luke smiles again. The NHS has done a grand job of providing clinicians with protective equipment; especially the transparent wipe clean visor I see before me. Reading Luke's mind will be easier for me than it is for him.

'No, thank you... Actually, could we avoid the supernatural?' thank goodness I managed to steer this twisty conversation away from my half-sister's half-sister.

Luke sits in silence in his chair with an expressionless face. I sit opposite him, fidgeting like an agitated ferret. I'd better say something before my stupor returns.

'So, err... Luke; Dr Schofield... I presume you've been a clinical psychologist for many years?' I use my best Jacquetta voice. If Heather taught me anything, it is to always give your best performance. Fuck what she says about lavender and mugwort; my older sister is everything to everyone (must stop swearing).

Luke remains silent. I wouldn't say he is staring at me, but he looks at me with half a smile. His jaws must hurt after eight hours of this open expression. Still, I imagine his pay band is higher than Diana and Jane's. Luke mirrors my steepled fingers, and I wonder if he is doing this to make me feel stupid. I am saved from this dupe when his hands briefly cover his face. Only a moment is needed for a professional of his calibre to readjust his fake smile. I wonder if I am the first telepathic patient Luke has tried to help. I must ask him later.

'It's just that, I presumed you had to train for several years to perfect your question asking technique.' The psychologist almost smirks at my cheeky words. If Luke did train for several years, he probably went to the same school as the Royal Guard. Luke does not flinch (must gift him a Busby when this is all over).

'I presumed that this would be a patient-centred meeting,' I give Luke one last try; my keeper will no doubt have reached the end of her forty winks on the other side of the door.

'That is three presumptions you have made, Pippa,' Luke allows his jaw a rest.

'It speaks! I thought you had sent me to Coventry,' I am still using Mummy's voice.

'Coventry?' Luke asks.

'Oh, it's just something Mummy used to say if she wasn't talking to someone. She's a royalist.'

'I'm familiar with the idiom, Pippa – didn't know it had anything to do with royalty, though. We are both here to have a conversation about you, and I am listening.'

I open my mouth to explain that Coventry had something to do with the civil war and that Mummy has spent her life conflicted between her royal roots and her oddities. Then I realise this is the time to start taking things seriously. This conversation is about me; that's why I was agitated. 'OK,' I say.

'You know, Pippa, there has been a huge increase in people suffering from mental health problems since the pandemic. You are not on your own; it is perfectly natural to experience feelings of despair and anxiety.'

'Everyone's talking about it.' I say cheerily. To be fair, psychologists have a tricky job; how does one slip murderous intent into the conversation?

'You're right; it has been all around us hasn't it? The news, social media, Covid has been on everyone's minds.'

'No, I meant mental health *that* is everywhere. I've been fine; I quite liked being isolated.' Damn this face mask! Dr Schofield misunderstood me.

'You are fine?' Luke doesn't believe me. I can't blame him, what kind of person sets out to murder her sister and her ex-best-friend on the orders of an apparition?

'I'm fine. You said so yourself, LUKE, it's only natural... you said it a few minutes ago.'

'It's only natural to seek out coping strategies, Pippa. Such as alcohol,' Luke tries to move the conversation along but now it is my turn to be silent. The psychologist had two choices here. Stare at me until I say something or until the appointment ends (whichever comes first). He could take a wild stab at something he read in the nursing notes.

Time is money in the NHS these days and so he asks; 'Do you ever feel unhappy?'

'Of course, I do, doesn't everyone? I'm angry right now!' (Shit, he said unhappiness, didn't he?)

'What would you say triggers your unhappiness?' Luke thinks I am a troublemaker, and he will not be swayed from unhappiness.

'What do you mean?'

'You were very unhappy when you arrived, Pippa. You were on your way to Pendle to run your sister over. What made you want to do that?'

'She...' I start crying. I want to explain everything, I do. I want to tell Luke about Sadie calling Heather the Pocahontas of Pendle and the green goddess. I want to tell him about Cassandra usurping Sadie's claim to The Peacock but I can't. Where inhalers free my throat constriction of tickles, my tear ducts conspire to block me.

'It's alright, Pippa,' Luke nods at the tissue dispenser.

'I've been feeling very guilty about crashing the jalopy. I'm not doing that again; I could have killed someone.'

'The best way to make sure that this kind of thing doesn't happen again is to understand why it happened and then put strategies in place to process those thoughts.'

I start to cry again; crocodile tears this time.

'Were you angry at your sister?'

'I presume that Heather will think or say something about the things I do and say.' Where did that come from? I haven't even had my brain scan yet.

'Why does this make you unhappy, Pippa?'

'Because Heather always disapproves of me!' Isn't it obvious?

'Do you always predict a negative judgement from your sister?' Luke asks.

'Yes, you saw her...' I try to think of an example from when Dr Schofield met Heather in the ward round. All I can think of is when I read Heather's mind, and she *knew* that I was a psychotic drinker.

'Does she actually, or do you *always think* Heather will be negative?'

'It's not just Heather that thinks badly of me,' I add this because I have to. My life has been spent condoning Heather's malfeasance.

'I don't think badly of you, and I haven't heard any evidence that Heather does either. Do you ever put this to the test?'

'Yes, it spreads. Heather phones me at work, and then the receptionist, Karen thinks I am a nuisance. Cassandra caused a load of trouble for Heather's dad and her... but at the time, we were school friends and...' I pause to check that Luke is still listening. Then I remember he probably read my notes and has heard what I told the nursing staff about my contretemps with Cassandra.

'So, Karen from work, Cassandra, and I believe you have had a few disagreements with Vickie, the night sister?'

'Yes, but none of this is my fault.'

'Does it need to be anyone's fault?'

'Well...'

'It seems that all these people, all these perceived enemies are just another version of Heather. What do you think, Pippa?'

'You're right,' I imagine my face being filmed right now. Filmed and made into a GIF for *the penny dropped*.

'But how do you know what Heather is thinking? Do you rely on your presumptions?'

'No! No, I can read Heather's mind.' Damn it, I did not want to talk about this – but only because I presume Luke will conclude that magical thinking is part of my illness.

'That's... not what I was expecting you to say, Pippa.' I knew it; Dr Schofield has never chanced upon a soothsayer before.

'It's not my fault, Luke. I didn't ask to have any special powers.'

'You know, I often get asked – by laymen as well as patients– if I can read minds.'

'And can you?' This was not what I was expecting Luke to say.

'No, not in the context I think you meant, you mentioned special powers... Is it telepathy Pippa? Or are we seeing people for what they truly are?' Luke pauses to take in my countenance. My mind is blown. I have waited all my life for an epiphany, and then several come all at once. I don't read minds; I just read people.

'How do you do it?'

'What? I mean, pardon… what do you mean?'

'Mind-reading.'

'I don't know how I do it. My ears start burning, and I start to think someone is talking about me.' Is Dr Schofield trying to learn from me?

'There's your evidence Pippa. Regardless of if the burning ears theory is true or not, how can you blame yourself for something that is being done to you?' Luke solves all my problems and wraps up our session in one sentence. I can go home now that I know none of this is my fault. I can prove it because Dr Schofield has gifted me a moment of clarity. Then Luke asks me to do something that I ignore instantly. 'Before our next session, I would like you to record any incidence of your negative presumptions, and then we can talk about them.'

Chapter Thirty-Three

I must say my mental health has improved over the last few days.

I do not read Heather's negativity towards me; I presume it. This pattern of thought has repeated throughout my nearly forty years. Unfortunately, I'm a bit confused about what Dr Schofield said (even though he was the person who gifted this glimmer of hope). Our session ended on a high, and I thought I could go home, but I couldn't remember why by the evening. I didn't manage to do my homework until something else happened during the night shift.

My counterpart inmate Andy returned to the lockup through the revolving door. This time he was angry, or a *risk to others.* Post sedation, we chatted in the dayroom. Andy had little to say about his restored custody but was all ears about my progress.

'I don't mean to burst your bubble, Pippa, but it sounds like one of our friends slipped you the truth serum before you spoke to that psychologist.' Andy either has the bullshit factor or is knowledgeable and well-versed about The Mary Shelley Unit. I consider that Andy has set the sirens off several times since our acquaintance, so he probably knows everything there is to know about the management of the mental. Yet, he said one thing which made me doubt him; *slipped me the truth serum.* Would I know if Dr Kershaw, Diana, Jane, or Vickie had administered this outdated intervention?

'I know what medication I'm on; I've finished the alcohol detox.' Is Andy getting at me? *Just another Heather;* I think I would know.

'I don't blame you for feeling defensive, Pippa. That's one of the side effects of truth drugs. You feel guilt for what you might have said. Tell me, do you feel as though you've done something you shouldn't have?'

'I do!' I don't know how Andy does it (and I can't believe I trusted these health professionals so quickly).

'It's not your fault, Pippa. The only thing you shouldn't have done is trust these bastards,' Andy sparks up a joint.

'You can't...' I was about to tell Andy that he can't do that in here, but our chat is cut short by Sister Vickie and her night shift friends. Then I really did do something I shouldn't have done, and I have no idea where it came from. Just when I thought I was getting better, and while the sirens were involved with my friend, I carved a long scar into my arm.

'Does it hurt, Pippa?' Vickie is dressing my wound. She described it as a superficial laceration yet asked me plenty of questions about suicidal thoughts.

'It's not too bad; how I'm feeling hurts more,' I say. Nurse Vickie was the first person to refute Sadie's existence; I don't know why I'm talking to her.

'I know that, Pippa. And I'm so sorry you're having a bad time... Someone once told me that they cut themselves to try and get a release,' Vickie soothes me; it is as though she is a different nurse.

'I can't apologise enough, Vickie,' I sob.

'I'm not the one with a big gash on my arm; you must be going through it, Pippa.' I read gentleness in Vickie's mind.

'You're very kind,' I was very wrong about Vickie. 'I suppose that's why I did it. I have been feeling trapped. I know we've all been trapped inside recently, but I think I might have trapped myself inside my own head.'

'That's understandable, Pippa... only, if you don't mind me asking, do you feel better or worse now?'

I look at the long bandage on my arm (which looks worse than it is). 'No, I don't feel better; I'm filled with remorse now.'

'I'd better put those razors in the safety box, just to be on the safe side. Would that be alright with you, Pippa?' Vickie is kind and buxom, not the cruel and combatant matron I first assumed. I've done my homework, and I am ready for my next session with Dr Schofield. I regret wasting the jumpsuit on my first appointment; with this long bandage and hairy legs, I could do with a coverall.

'And Vickie was not negative at all. I didn't get one hateful vibe off her when she discovered my contraband hair removal kit,' I am sure I shall be Luke's star pupil today. I wonder if he's married.

'OK, Pippa, I did not mean for you to test out your negative presumptions by doing yourself harm. You must know that,' Luke says.

'Oh, I do know that. I am pleased about it in a way because I thought Vickie disliked me, and she was so kind when I cut myself...'

'Vickie is not your sister, though, and I didn't intend for you to engage in these harmful safety behaviours.' Luke asks me about two things, smoking and cutting, and it turns out that Andy was the catalyst for my misbehaviour. 'In the ward round, you said that you didn't want to ask a lot of different people the same question, so why are you turning to Andy for advice? He's got his own problems, surely.'

'So, you want me to just listen to your solace?' I have almost got it.

'Not exactly, Pippa. I'm trying to support you to improve your coping strategies so that you can help yourself when I'm not there. If you have a robust set of skills in your mental toolbox, you are more likely to stay healthy.' Luke wants to say *you are less likely to murder* your sister; it is on the tip of his tongue.

'How can I stay healthy when they've stopped

my vitamin prescription?' I say (these people are obsessed with health).

'That's because you don't need them now that you're sober, Pippa. You should congratulate yourself.'

'I've managed to swap one addiction for another,' I *am* pleased with myself.

'NO!' Dr Schofield puts me straight; he laughs, though.

The next few weeks are difficult. I slowly improve, but it is hard work for the staff and for me. I was transferred to the female open ward. Andy is no longer present to tempt me with maladaptive coping strategies.

I must say, Ben has been the perfect doting boyfriend. He has arrived on time for every single visiting hour. During the day, he breaks his back raising renovations at The Peacock. Then after a quick shower, he reports for duty as my one and only. Ben tells me he has a surprise planned for my first day leave next week (all being well). He seems pleased about something; he's either proposing or letting me watch a romantic comedy.

Mummy and Heather, of course, have visited me. Neither will pass up the opportunity to bring the drama. They alternate days and variations, Mummy visiting with John and Heather visits with Rhys. My cordial interactions with Heather are noted down as a sign of my recovery. I have managed to keep any fugue state at bay. Actually, I haven't felt overly agitated since before Sadie was on duty in the intensive care ward. And I've figured out that if I do not mention Sadie, then my conversations with the nursing staff are 'normal'. The ward I was transferred to is Jane's substantive workplace, and she introduced me to all her friends. She chuckled and said I should call them *colleagues.* Ever since then, I have greeted the nursing staff (there's so many of them) with 'Good morning, colleague.' I am a hit and they have been wonderful.

Speaking of not mentioning Sadie, my chats with Dr Schofield continue. He eventually tricked me into talking about my half-sister's half-sister by using Jung in his warm-up questions.

'I'm glad you asked Luke. I'm an introvert usually... When I thought Cassandra was trying to take Ben off me I didn't talk to anyone about it but when Sadie is around, I'm an extravert,' I am smiling but Luke appears serious.

'I've been wondering when you would mention Sadie. Do you remember our first appointment? You asked me to steer clear of supernatural topics. Are you now open to talking about her?'

'Sadie isn't supernatural! Goodness no! She visited me just after lockdown ended; I hadn't seen her for years.'

Dr Schofield gives me his 'listening' face.

'Ben saw her, you should ask him.'

Dr Schofield thumbs through my computer-ised notes, and I hope that Heather's report about Sadie's demise has vanished.

'It's Mummy and Heather who are the witches, not Sadie.'

'Your mother and sister are quite powerful characters, aren't they?' Luke has assumed I used the word *witch* as an adjective.

'Heather, yes, but Mummy? If she actually was a witch, she would be one of those weak ones; locked inside her house with her cat.' I must refute the notion that I believe in magical thinking.

'We'll come back to the witchcraft metaphor if that's OK with you, Pippa?'

Damn it.

'Some introverts who grow up with an extra-vert sibling attribute the extravert's outward per-sonality as a negative. But the thing we must re-member is that we are talking about personalities.'

'So, it isn't Heather's fault?' Great, this means I've been the insipid sibling all my life, and it's my fault for being shy, not Heather's fault for being brash.

'There is no fault to be had, Pippa. None of us can help what we are – but we can all employ dam-age limitation,' Luke sort of told me off for trying to blame Heather for everything that has gone to shit in my life. 'Let me put something out there, Pippa. I think you're ready. Is it possible that you imagined your mother and sister to be witches be-cause you felt left out of their relationship? How could you possibly be part of their family if you, yourself are not a witch?'

'How do you know I'm not a witch? I didn't know I had an alcohol problem...' I force the words out of my choking throat.

'We'll come to that... the alcohol. But before we do, I want to ask you something. Is it possible that Sadie appeared in your life, real or imagined, because she is not a witch, like your mother or sister and therefore a positive allied influence?'

I'm so confused. Sadie was talking about witchcraft during her invisible night duty. She was also smoking cannabis right under the smoke alarm. Luke has a point though... I did need jollying along when Sadie turned up. Lockdown was ending, and I didn't even know if I could stay in my home. Luke hasn't even asked me if I'm afraid of being uprooted yet; I'm sure he'll get to it. He is Luke Skywalker.

Chapter Thirty-Four

The next few appointments with Dr Schofield feel like I am really getting somewhere. Dr Carnegie is perfectly happy to put the medical model to one side (bar a cursory prescription), she allows Luke free rein on my brain (the scanning of which came back inconclusive).

Dr Schofield suggests that as I have already taken my thoughts and feelings 'out of the box', we put them back in one by one. First, we must process and make sense of them.

I agree to this strategy, although some of what's in my head must remain secret. They may well have scanned my brain, but the rest is private.

Surprisingly the asthma diagnosis came up first. Luke elicited a confession that I had spent my formative years one year behind at school with a tickle in my throat; often too scared to open my mouth (as this would induce a coughing fit). It seems impossible to conclude that my mother neglected my respiratory health, even if we confronted her about it. I did disclose a memory of Heather filling a bowl with steaming water... Half an hour I sat in front of that wet cloud watching floating herbs with a towel over my head.

Discussing Sadie's 'visits' led to working out how much I had been drinking. Bless Dr Schofield, he avoided confronting me about Sadie's reality and focused on why I associated Sadie with misbehaviour. I perceived alcohol as a clandestine pursuit for many reasons. I had observed Mummy drinking alone when I was a child. My mother is blameless here; my proclivity to copy others' behaviour added concealing alcohol to my coping strategies, using it to turn my negative thoughts off and make me feel normal. I stole it from my mother's pub because I felt left out and that she owed me something. I kept my gin hobby a secret (even from myself) because I wanted to be like Heather. She can cope in any or all situations (I had presumed). Dr Schofield views that my recovery from this maladaptive habit will be a success as I am motivated to change my habits (only because my boyfriend will be running The Peacock – I'm not stupid). Luke promises that with more therapy, I shall learn that no one is perfect (not even Heather). That it is impossible to turn off negative thoughts completely, but they can be managed by building on positivity in the present. Damage limitation is possible, and I may, in the future be able to 'appropriately' enjoy a glass of wine.

No further stupors or a fugue state leads Dr Schofield to conclude my presentation was due to anxious avoidance. Dr Carnegie disagrees; she has labelled me with schizoaffective disorder (Erica made me feel special when she explained that this is quite rare). Luke advises me this divergence is not a sign of discord between psychology and the medical model. Then he advised me to 'be careful'; Dr Schofield even goes as far as saying that I 'shouldn't be on my own'. I assure him that Ben has replaced Grace Poole and promised to 'take care of me'. Dr Schofield thumbs through my medical notes for Bronte's nurse, and I read that no one knows what is really wrong with me.

'I want to talk about something you said when you were first admitted to the PICU downstairs,' Luke says on this midsummer and humid morning.

'The lockup?' I correct him.

'You told the nursing staff that your mother is descended from the royal family.' Luke waits for my response, which is fortuitous because I need time to think.

'Did I?' (Did I?) 'Don't forget, Dr Schofield, they said I was drunk when the police brought me here.'

'And so, your mind may not have formed the memories.'

'I meant I can't remember much about it.' (I did not know that about alcohol.)

'You did, Pippa. Nurse Vickie was not the only person to record your words in your notes. Do you believe me?' Luke sits forwards and studies my face (half of which is covered by a mask).

'Yes, of course, I believe you and Vickie!' I

don't... This could well have been Sadie playing tricks in the night. Then it vaguely creeps back to me that I remember Mummy saying something about where her name comes from.

'Obviously, I was overexcited the night I was admitted.' I read Luke, and he agrees. 'I was trying to escape, wasn't I? How better to go AWOL than to claim that royal blood courses through my veins and therefore should not be here. No offence.'

'None taken, and I've heard more successful ways of breaking out.' Luke laughs, and I wonder if he has treated Andy.

'You can't have this one, Dr Schofield, I'm sorry. Mummy used to tell me that she is descended from Jacquetta of Luxembourg.' (I cannot read Luke's response.) 'Jacquetta was part of the nobility, and her daughter married some English King, or other; in the *olden days*.' I speak to Luke as though he is uneducated; I need to throw him off the scent of Googling Jacquetta of Luxembourg.

'It's interesting that you compared your mother to a witch,' Luke says (Damn it).

'I didn't, I'm not the deluded one. Mummy was named after her great-great how-ever-many grandmothers.' As I say this, Dr Schofield scribbles something in his notebook. I read that he plans to write a scholarly article about my complex delusional system. I should have told Vickie about Jacquetta's lineage, if anyone deserves a perk of the job, it's her.

'Does all this lead back to Heather in some

way?' Luke asks.

'Don't tell me Mummy is just another Heather?'

'Well, who picked your name, Epiphany?'

'Heather did,' I say.

'Heather chose your name?' I thought that Luke had read my mind, but his eyes are bulging like a teenage peeping Tom.

'Yes, really; my older sister chose my stupid name. Everyone thought that Mummy experienced a revelation when I was born but no, Heather was allowed to pick my name as compensation for my arrival.'

'That's really interesting, Pippa. I think we may have discovered the starting point of your troubles.'

'Since birth?' I am doomed.

'Not exactly, you perceive your name to be something negative and therefore Heather intended you to be hurt.'

'Well, yes. It's not a name! It's a... thingy.'

'It's unusual and probably made you stand out when you were at school,' (I suffer flashbacks of Cassandra befriending me on that very notion.) 'Maybe you disliked it because you prefer to slip into the background?'

'Yes, I used to wish I was invisible.' I think back to Sadie asking me what my superpower is. 'I just don't like it, Dr Schofield. I prefer to be called Pippa. That's all.'

'How do you think Heather felt when you

were born?'

'Left out.' I knew Luke would make me play the *'if the shoe was on the other foot'* game (and I'm still waiting for the 'uprooted' analogy).

'So, is it possible that Heather made you feel left out because she felt left out?'

'Yes! Dr Schofield, thank you so much, I am not at fault here, am I? Everything is Heather's fault. I can go home now!' The gratitude I feel right now is immense. The psychologist has listened to my every word and concluded I'm not to blame.

'Not exactly, don't forget what we talked about, Pippa. No one is perfect including your sister. I meant we should consider how Heather felt when you were born, she was a child herself.'

'She was a teenager when I was born,' I add.

'A teenager then... The point is that your response to Heather's crisis of confidence produced your schema. Heather gave you a name you dislike, and this made you wary of possible hatred; be it from your sister or anyone.' Luke appears to have reached the conclusion of therapy, what he said does kind of sound like me.

'Can I go home now?' I say.

'Maybe Dr Carnegie will discharge you soon, but I don't think you should terminate your treatment.'

Like everyone, I was physically incarcerated for over a year. I coped well with this because I had been trapped by introversion all my life. I was frightened of life, frightened of love. I picked the wrong man so many times because I worried what Heather would think. Now that I'm ready to be an extravert; Luke wants to keep boring me?

'Pippa, when you are discharged from here, I will refer you to a psychologist in the community. You have a lot of work to do about grief. You found out that your father died while you were in hospital and will need to work through your feelings.'

I agree, although I shan't grieve for Maddox; I hardly knew the man. It's Sadie that I'll miss. If she *is* imaginary (the condition of my discharge) then I will be devastated.

Chapter Thirty-Five

I have slept better these past few nights, which is really cutting into my reading time. I miss Agatha... I miss Sadie... I miss home.

The only reason I am unable to read during the day is Lucy. After seeing Ben visit (and noting how devoted we are), she no longer saw me as a threat to her liaison with Andy. We became friends, and she tried to get me to join her 'I hate Andy' club. I manage to resist on the grounds that she might change her mind and things would be awkward. Annie joined without hesitation, but I think she was desperate for the company. Apparently, Dr Schofield recommended she divorce her husband. 'Don't trust that fucking psychologist. And don't trust Andy either, he's a plant,' Annie was clearly unready for her transfer. Lucy talks at length about her obsession with Andy, and I understand completely.

Ward round comes around again and because of my exemplary behaviour, I am treated to an overnight stay at home. Heather promises to bring something tasty around for our evening meal (she assumes she is invited). I read *that won't be necessary* in Ben's mind.

'I'm so excited for you to see the pub, Pippa.

You will absolutely love it when you see how much work I've done... I'm having today off though, to take care of you.' Ben is very pleased with his achievements. Also, he has not failed to notice how much work I put into today's outfit (I am looking forward to getting home).

We go round The Peacock's refurbishment on this fair and fragile morning. Ben was not lying; he has proved his redundancy futile and gutted the entire ground floor of the building. I am astounded at how light and weirdly bigger The Peacock looks without its fusty furnishings (Ben's DIY ferocity is proof of his ardour for our new life).

'So, if you can imagine... in your mind's eye, Pippa, the bar will be here and the toilets over there.' Ben has a good nose for this sort of thing, never in the history of The Peacock has the bar area been free from public embarrassments.

'You've done an awesome job, Ben. I'm so proud of you,' I hug my lover, and I mean every word. I am happy, because Ben makes me forget everything. A lifetime of worrying about what Heather might think has ended. It doesn't matter that he is seven years and two months younger than me because I am a good seven years or more away from the menopause (and in the right light, I haven't aged since high school). Dr Schofield helped me work out my obsession with hormonal imbalance was yet another reflection of Heather. She is all things to all people, and I tried to copy her middle-aged woes. The mood swings I suffered were another story, but at least I am fully fertile (should the need arise).

'I thought we could get a takeaway tonight, and then we will have each other's full attention,' Ben slips his arms around my waist.

'Thank you, I'm not ready to go out. I just want to be upstairs in my... our flat.' I submit to my reclusive tendencies.

'I know, Pippa. That's why I've arranged a surprise for you.'

'A surprise?' I am rooted to the spot. Is this a test? Am I about to repeat my stupor?

'Don't worry, it's someone you know, and if you don't like it, she's promised to go back home. No questions asked. I'll be here, Pippa to take care of you. It was actually your friend Lucy from the ward's idea – well, part of it.'

God help me; has Mad Annie followed me home?

'There's the doorbell. I'll let her in,' I read *don't worry* in Ben's mind. He must have started talking to himself while I've been away.

My mouth dries up in the short space of time that Ben takes to unlock the door that can't be unlocked. Mummy messaged me to say that her keys are missing (again), and she will pop over when Patrice gives up their whereabouts. Heather agreed to visit next time I am home. Sadie is a figment of my imagination. I wonder who this can be... I pray Ben has not invited Karen round as I pour myself a glass of water; I'm allergic to alcohol and can't be persuaded that easily.

'Hello, Pippa. Do you remember me?' It is Mrs Sparks, and this time she is the timid one. She carries a big holdall and for a moment, I think that India Kitten is inside. 'I've come to give you a cut and blow dry; your boyfriend thought you might like it.' Mrs Sparks and Ben grin at me with conspiratorial hope.

Mrs Sparks (Jessica) is a part-time mobile hairdresser. And Ben (on the say-so of Lucy) thought it a good idea that she attend to my crowning frizz during my home leave. It turns out that Lucy figures appearance to be a sure-fire way of expediting discharge from The Mary Shelley Unit (which is why she looks the way she does). Although this serendipitous meeting has nothing to do with my treatment, I must write something in the suggestion box on the ward. The NHS would save a lot of money if pampering was given out on prescription.

Jessica and I disagree on one point only; when I ask to darken my hair to a jet black or brunette, she warns me this is a 'big commitment'. Apart from that, we get on very well. Jessica is full of tales about India Kitten, and she does not say no when I ask if I can visit. India Kitten looks to have grown from her photographs (none of which feature the Sparks' child), and I read that she is happy (even though her name has been changed to Mrs Patch).

Jessica is a whizz with the scissors. She has many potions with her, including a powerful purple liquid to prevent my hair from 'looking brash'. I presume no ill humours in this woman's vibe, and I watch her in the mirror tackling my thatch with a hairdryer and round brush. Here we go round my frizz and flax on a day release from psychiatry.

Jessica appears to be enjoying this; I imagine coaxing my hair into submission gives her a sense of achievement. She tells me a story (without naming any names) about a woman with long, dark, unyielding hair as strong as steel and as glorious as her face. I miss Sadie.

'Wow!' Ben is summoned to see the success of Jessica's efforts. I read pride (I was hoping for desire).

'Do you love it, Ben?' Jessica asks.

'I look awesome, don't I?' I say.

'I love it,' Ben hugs me and laughs at me at the same time.

'Mrs Sparks? I'm Jacquetta...' Mummy appears like the keeper of all keys. I don't know how she recognises my new hairdresser (Heather's descriptions must be very vivid).

'Hello, yes, I'm Mrs Sparks,' Jessica says.

'I'm Jacquetta... your next appointment...Move, Pippa. Are you better, by the way?' Mummy fills the chair I vacate, pulling hairpins from her hair. Jessica frowns at her social media booking system, I read that she promises to never answer the phone when driving ever again.

Ben did not propose last night, and we are on our way back to The Mary Shelley Unit for a meeting with Dr Carnegie.

'I am so sorry about yesterday, Pippa. I have no clue how your mother knew Mrs Sparks was doing your hair.'

'It's not your fault, Ben.' We both laugh.

'Did you hear Mrs Sparks? She said your hair is a pleasure to work with, and you should definitely arrange another appointment in a couple of months,' Ben's eyes are on the road; I remember reading *not you* in Mrs Sparks' eyes about Mummy.

'I'm glad you're feeling better, Pippa; and that you agree to the aftercare that we've set up. It is great news for us that you have a supportive home life,' Dr Carnegie is pleased to see me return safe and well after one night at home.

'Yes, she definitely does,' Ben squeezes my hand.

'Even though some of the restrictions have been relaxed, we can no longer afford the luxury of extended leave periods in and out of hospital. You understand that, don't you Pippa? It's because of the potential for isolation.'

'Yes?' Is Dr Carnegie going to isolate me in the

lockup again?

'So, I've decided to discharge you from the ward today, but admit you to the home treatment team.'

'That's great,' Ben is beaming.

'Are they going to move into my flat with me? Will I have to meet more people?' I dread more people.

'I'm afraid you will have some changes to the personnel involved in your care, Pippa. Dr Schofield will transfer you to the community psychologist, and you will meet a new team of nurses. I think you're ready, Pippa. It's good to move on... and no, they won't need to live with you... they will either do phone contacts or home visits when needed.'

'I'll be safe?'

'You'll be quite safe, Pippa. They are all professionals like the staff here; they're very strict about infection control.'

I didn't mean that.

Although I imagine a grand farewell, with nurses and patients queuing up to wave me off, my final moments at The Mary Shelley Unit are an anti-climax. Dr Carnegie *would* shake my hand, but the less contact the better (in this context). I should send the nursing staff a box of teabags or something (I expect they are all fastidiously healthy and never eat chocolates).

Ben and I are instructed to wait in reception.

Through the internal glass, I notice Andy waving at me furiously. No one is looking, so Ben opens the door out onto the courtyard. From behind the mulberry bush, Andy has a goodbye message for me. 'I never want to fucking see you in here ever again. I mean it Pippa, don't you ever have another episode.' I think he meant well.

After what seems like seventy-two hours, a pharmacist wearing a forensic suit pops out of a door in the lobby area and hands me a bag of tablets like a sanitised drug deal.

I wonder which romantic comedy we will watch tonight.

Chapter Thirty-Six

Heather has come to visit me at The Peacock. She actually spends more time with me than she does Mummy during these past few weeks, and this is *not bad*. 'I agree with you about Cassandra, Pippa. Everyone knows that vampires and witches don't mix.' Heather offers a fine *Sadie* voice and is all things to all people; as am I (we are simpatico). 'PIPSQUEAK! You drifted off there... Are you sure they're not overmedicating you?' Heather clicks her fingers in my face.

'No, I'm just taking a common or garden mood stabiliser... What did you say?'

'I said I agree with you about Cassandra. I've always known she's a total bitch.'

Shit.

I misheard her.

'I'm glad she's true to her word about being a silent partner. Massive congratulations, by the way, Pippa. Your young man has done a fine job of these renovations; he's a keeper.'

'I always thought you didn't like Ben?' I say.

'I don't even like my own husband very much, Pippa, but I've learnt not to *need* Rhys, just to want him.' Heather's eyes shine hazel, and she offers a smile. Our sisterly connection sounds as good as Earl Grey and lemon on an August day. Heather luxuriates in the lounge area of The Peacock for a while longer. Having completed her two-hour shift of titivating wine glasses and highball tumblers she pats the seat at the side of her for me to join her. 'Are you absolutely sure about tomorrow?'

It is seventy-two days since I took annual leave from my job counting sums. Mr Bland has shown a great deal of understanding of my situation. Aside from his fear of industrial tribunals, Heather and Mummy have his ear, and I am to return tomorrow (at whatever time suits me) because I will benefit from the routine. Nothing has changed since I last worked; it will be different but the same (and hopefully better).

My community treatment continues without a snag; I am learning more about mental health and wellbeing. The community psychologist is even better than Luke Skywalker. She has a weird hybrid name; I think her surname is really her first name. We will meet on Skype once a week until I am strong enough to be discharged. So far, Dr Morgana has picked up on my 'different voices'; she reassures me that everyone does this to some extent (you wouldn't swear in front of a child, for example). She plans to spend some time forcing me to talk about why I do this, starting with exploring why I favour pop culture from Heather's era rather than my own. This is to be our first disagreement. When Dr Morgana asks me if I remember popular music from the year I was 16, I tell her I'm not that innocent. The next time we met, she identified mistakes in my thought process when I explained that Mummy sacrificed a lot for me. This time, it was I that disagreed with the psychologist; I know Mummy gave up a lot of things for me because she was always reminding me of the fact. Always. Still, I made an agreement with Andy never to return to The Mary Shelley Unit, and so my chats with Dr Morgana shall continue.

Rightly or wrongly, Heather put herself forwards as my sponsor. I accepted her offer because she seemed so excited about it, insisting that we should both 'see how long we can go without wine'. Heather is even convinced that one day in the future, we shall see a dry Jacquetta. It hardly seems worth it in Mummy's case, but I'm no expert. This arrangement has worked so far because I cannot lie to Heather, and she cannot lie to me. Not even if we tried (we can read each other like a book) and for the first time, I see Heather's competitive nature as zealous. She means no harm, she does what she will.

My eyes are open to the possibility of relapse, or as Heather put it 'a wobble'. What happens to me next will happen anyway. Thinking about the past or future will not change either of those time shifts. Things are so much easier now that my block of fear has dissolved. I no longer dread unjustifiable accusations of failure because I'm funny, fair, and nearly forty. Should anyone start their sentence with *'what you should do is'* I'll be ready for them. No longer a simpering people pleaser; assertive Pippa is the real epiphany.

I have to admit that this feeling of hope was gifted to me by my half-sister's half-sister. I have been asked what my secret is, how am I always so jovial? Partly, this is down to Ben, but secretly this is down to Sadie (or possibly me). Mostly, this secret is private.

Sadie visits me occasionally, but not to encourage surreptitious sessions or even to cheer me with sideways sneers.

'Please tell me you're not going to wear that?' Sadie watches me open another discount delivery.

'But it's leopard print,' I stand my ground.

'No, it isn't, Pippa, it's a t-shirt with a print of a leopard in the middle. You can't wear it, because it will make you look like Heather.'

'You can't say that!' I say, but Sadie is gone and Heather arrives.

'Oh my goodness, Pippa, thank you! Oh, it's beautiful,' Heather holds the t-shirt up to herself in the mirror.

'Just a little something to say thank you for all the support you've given me over the past few months.' These moments of chance roll off my tongue with ease around Heather these days.

'It's like we know one another really well now,' Heather says. She knows I tried to kill her, she must do. Psychiatrists don't keep that kind of riskiness confidential. Still, not discussing my murderous streak has fallen into the unspoken area of our bond, and Heather has chosen to compartmentalise this memory with wispiness (while holding onto the belief that I was driving to Pendle that day for care and consolation).

As for Cassandra, she has kept to her word, and both she and Tristan have stayed away. After almost making me sink, I managed to swim to the surface. If Cassandra doesn't want to be my friend that's her problem, not mine. She is more than capable of finding another female to push around in her dogstooth swimming costume (unfortunately, she has a daughter). I don't feel guilty for her banishment; Cassandra's share in The Peacock should have been Sadie's share. I was not the cause of Tristan's car crash; mental illness is not something I asked for.

In a few years, we'll be able to buy Cassandra out. I say we, because Ben and I complete the circle now. Ben no longer says, 'I'll take care of it, Pippa.' He says with eyes that reveal he has always known I'm the one; 'I love you.' And I love him too. It must have been lonely for Ben the first time he spoke those words to me; I stared at him in fear. Did I really think he wanted to kill me? I've reached halfway, and I've already found what I'm looking for.

Am I still paranoid? Yes, of course, I am; but I can recognise it now, and we extraverts thrive on talking things through. A couple of days ago, I accused Ben of only being with me because of The Peacock. I didn't mention it at first, but a dark cloud descended on my mood and thoughts, and I began to start with intrusions that Ben had been stealing from me. I couldn't stop myself from telephoning him while I was at work to ask if he had stolen the jalopy (ridiculous really, my car was not worth picking up from the police pound, and I knew it had been scrapped). We talked it through when I arrived home. Ben understood why I might be thinking this way, because The Peacock is something belonging to my family. All the poor lamb could do was shower me with plenty of reassurance and offer the theory that time will prove his devotion (he didn't use the word devotion, but I was sold on the idea). The following day, Ben was not sure that I was sure, and so he planned a surprise weekend away to Pembrokeshire. He has a theory that I need to visit the location where my father (and Sadie) disappeared. Thankfully, this trip is sometime in the future because The Peacock has put a dampener on any merriment for Ben and me for the foreseeable. No matter, I like being isolated.

During the lost year, I was frumpy, fair, and forgotten. Here I went round the mulberry bush and tonight, we reopen The Peacock.

'Jacquetta and John are walking over the road,

Pippa... hide the sweet sherry!' Heather winks at me.

'Welcome,' Ben opens the entrance to The Peacock; Jacquetta and John shake hands with him. They glory in the turquoise and (other subtle) colours of Ben's compliance in the new decor (Cassandra didn't get a look in on the colour charts). I wave Mummy over to the bookshelf I have installed in one of the old fireplace alcoves. I see this contrivance as a quirky community library. (Although Mummy tells me she has never-ever seen spaces such as an old telephone box used for the lending and borrowing of paperbacks; what an absolute NIGHTMARE, Pippa!)

It is here, next to my book tower and amongst the plush upholstery that I dream of hosting book launches – or a book club at least (Mrs Sparks is fully on board with this idea).

Ben is at home behind the bar, taking care of everyone's immediate needs. He winks at me and points at my empty tumbler. I see little point in swallowing gallons of soft liquids; I don't like the taste of sparkling elderflower *that much.* Ben intimates he will take care of me from his background, yet present position.

Oswald arrives and he, Mummy, and John give lubricated speeches about now being *the right time* to hand over The Peacock.

I notice Heather frantically looking at her watch and scrolling her phone screen. 'Is everything alright, Heather? Didn't Rhys say he would be late?' I can now ask Heather personal questions without her returning a bitter retort.

'Yes, he's on his way. He went to look at Leeds University with Fabian today, didn't he?' Heather whispers. I always smile when I hear my youngest nephew's name.

'It's not that, Pippa. I've done something naughty.' Heather put her top lip over her bottom lip almost as Sadie would. 'Do not say anything to Oswald, please; he'll be over in a minute...'

'I won't... you'd better put some shades on though, Heather. Your eyes are hazel... what have you done?'

'I sent a box of lavender and lemon balm biscuits to Cassandra earlier today.'

'I didn't know you could flavour biscuits with lavender,' I know my face says *tastes like air freshener*.

'Witches do,' Heather says.

'What? I mean, pardon.'

'I said, no harm done, Epiphany. I was just trying to find out how they went down by checking Cassandra's social media... Obviously, I can't ask her...' If Cassandra ate any of Heather's ladyfingers she may not be able to answer even if Heather did telephone her. Heather keeps the lines of communication open with our adversary via avenues of healing. This is Heather's version of killing with kindness (kinder than a tonne of steel).

'Do as you will Heather.' This is awesome; the peace I feel right now is immense. Finally, after all this time, Heather is listening to me.

'And you, Pippa,' Heather puts her arm around my shoulder and squeezes me to her. It dawned on me last week that I am not the only one with cause to grieve for Sadie; Heather was her actual half-sister. Still, there is room enough in our unspoken agreement for ill winds.

It is time to end our family tribute. Ben has made a fuss across the entrance of The Peacock with the intention of cutting the ribbon. Once divided, strangers shall be permitted to pass (on the understanding that they part with brass in exchange for muck). I never knew he had it in him to be so symbolic.

My sister saved me from the ducking stool.

This is the way we do no harm, on a bright and florid full moon.

Acknowledgements

Thank you, dear reader for listening to Pippa's story; if you enjoyed My Half-Sister's Half-Sister, please tell your friends. If you didn't like it, tell no one.

Thank you to Alison at https://www.alisonproof-reader.com/ for the lifesaving grammar skills.

Thank you to Lindsay McKinnon at https://www.theatreofthemindproductions.co.uk/ for her unbelievable spoken word interpretations available in the audio book format of this text (release date 2022).

Thank you to Kerry Howarth at https://www.instagram.com/kerry_draws/ for the beautiful cover illustration.

Thank you to Deborah Miles of Against the Flow Press for the fabulous cover reveal https://againsttheflowpress.blogspot.com/

Thank you to the 19th century female inmates of HMP Wakefield for the mulberry bush rhyme.

Thank you to Jean Rhys for the intertextual reference; Mr Blank (*Good Morning, Midnight*) became Pippa's Mr Bland. I acknowledge any other intertextual references; if you know, you know (Bronte, Hardy, Love, Walker, *et al.*).

Big love to Mr and Mrs Cavanagh for your support and inspiration, especially the eye patch/Oswald story (also, thank you to Tyler Holt for telling Alex the eye-patch info in the first place).

Massive thank you to Janaki and Neil for listening to me repeating myself about the best book I've ever written.

Big embarrassments to my daughter, Alicia – she works as an accountant and doesn't mind me saying 'sums'.

Thank you to the unknown estate agent who left several voicemails on my mobile, it was only when I eventually answered I was able to tell her she had the wrong number. There is no 'Mr Sparks' living at my house; but thank you for the name.

Thank you to Lee Schofield and Vickie Kershaw for answering my post on Facebook (a competition about names).

Massive huge thank you to one of my best friends Claire for gifting me the name 'Epiphany' (Pippa for short); you inspire me more than you know, Claire.

Thank you to my sister-in-law Kerry for the chat about enjoying books with a 'different' plot.

Thank you to my husband, Mr Henthorn for giving

me the courage to write (and the four day holiday you took in June with your brother really helped me get the book's word count up).

Thank you to Sophie Willan for appearing on BBC2's *Between the Covers*- my character Pippa agrees; when heartbroken, read an Agatha Christie.

Thank you to Gary Neville for being in the same school year as me at Elton High School (I don't think I need permission to include his name in my character Andy's delusions – but just in case, thank you Gary Neville ex Manchester United and England footballer and pundit).

About the Author

Samantha Henthorn was born in Bury (UK) in 1970something. As a child, she read Roald Dahl, as a teenager she read Stephen King. In 2005, Samantha went blind in her left eye and was subsequently diagnosed with MS. Nine years later Samantha accepted ill health retirement from her twenty-year nursing career. Samantha has one daughter, one dog, and one husband. Most of her time is spent minding her own business (though, she is thrilled to learn that someone has enjoyed her books). Follow Samantha on social media, or her blog: https://samanthahenthorn-findstherightwords.wordpress.com/. Join Samantha's mailing list: https://landing.mailerlite.com/webforms/landing/d0q2h7

The Curmudgeon Avenue Series (six-part series)
1962 (an uplifting tale of 1960s Lancashire)
Piccalilly (a Remembrance Day story)
Quirky Tales to Make Your Day
What we did During Lockdown

Printed in Great Britain
by Amazon

28982951R00162